PRAISE FOR THE CHASTITY RILEY SERIES

WINNER of the CWA Crime in Translation Dagger

'A distinctive voice, and a flawed but compelling protagonist. This is vintage Buchholz – style and sass and St Pauli' Will Carver

'Fans of the series will love this, and for those of you who haven't met Chastity yet, bringing us back to the beginning with *The Acapulco* and *The Kitchen* gives you the perfect reason to get reading. So what are you waiting for? Heartily recommended' Jen Med's Book Reviews

'Simone packs punch after punch into her short, snappy and pacy chapters, with injections of entries from an unknown source, *The Kitchen* had me HOOKED and wanting more! I flew through the pages of this book, lapping up the darkness, the moral questions, and Chastity, who has become one of my favourite female protagonists!' The Reading Closet

'Reading Buchholz is like walking on firecrackers … a truly unique voice in crime fiction' Graeme Macrae Burnet

'Such a revelation' Laura Lippman

'If Philip Marlowe and Bernie Gunther had a literary love child, it might just explain Chastity Riley – Simone Buchholz's tough, acerbic, utterly engaging central character' William Ryan

'Caustic, incisive prose. A street-smart, gutsy heroine. A timely and staggeringly stylish thriller' Will Carver

'A stylish, whip-smart thriller' Russel McLean

'A must-read, stylish and highly original take on the detective novel, written with great skill and popping with great characters' Judith O'Reilly

THE KITCHEN

ABOUT THE AUTHOR

Simone Buchholz was born in Hanau in 1972. At university, she studied philosophy and literature, worked as a waitress and a columnist, and trained to be a journalist at the prestigious Henri-Nannen-School in Hamburg. In 2016, she was awarded the Crime Cologne Award as well as runner-up in the German Crime Fiction Prize for *Blue Night*, which was number one on the KrimiZEIT Best of Crime List for months. The critically acclaimed *Beton Rouge*, *Mexico Street*, *Hotel Cartagena* and *River Clyde* all followed in the Chastity Riley series. *Mexico Street* won the German Crime Fiction Prize in 2019 and *Hotel Cartagena* won the CWA Crime in Translation Dagger in 2022. *The Acapulco* (2023) marked the beginning of the Chastity Reloaded series. Simone lives in Sankt Pauli, in the heart of Hamburg, with her son.

ABOUT THE TRANSLATOR

Rachel Ward is a freelance translator of literary and creative texts from German and French to English, specialising in crime fiction and books for children and young adults. Having studied modern languages at the University of East Anglia, she went on to complete UEA's MA in Literary Translation. She has previously translated Simone Buchholz's *Blue Night*, *Beton Rouge*, *Mexico Street*, *Hotel Cartagena* and *River Clyde* for Orenda Books. Her translation of *Hotel Cartagena* won the 2022 CWA Crime Fiction in Translation Dagger award. Her non-fiction interests include history, politics, art, journalism and travel. Follow Rachel on Twitter @FwdTranslations, Bluesky as @racheltranslates.bsky.social and Instagram as @racheltranslates.

THE KITCHEN

SIMONE BUCHHOLZ

TRANSLATED BY RACHEL WARD

**ORENDA
BOOKS**

Orenda Books
16 Carson Road
West Dulwich
London SE21 8HU
www.orendabooks.co.uk

First published in German as *Knastpralinen* by Suhrkamp Verlag AG, Berlin, in 2023, in a
revised version of the text, reworked by the author, of the edition published in 2010 by
Droemer/Knaur, Munich, under the same title.

This edition first published in the United Kingdom by Orenda Books 2024
Copyright © Suhrkamp Verlag Berlin 2023
English translation © Rachel Ward 2024

A catalogue record for this book is available from the British Library.

ISBN 978-1-916788-07-7
eISBN 978-1-916788-08-4

Typeset in Garamond by www.typesetter.org.uk

Printed and bound by CPI Group (UK) Ltd, Croydon CR0 4YY

For sales and distribution, please contact info@orendabooks or visit
www.orendabooks.co.uk.

So, tell me now:
How far would you go for your girlfriends?

The room is fully tiled, in a pale, matt grey. Cool. Modern. The units and worksurfaces, the pots, the pans and the bowls are stainless steel. In the centre is an island consisting of two massive gas hobs with four rings each. To the left, set into the floor: a drain.

There are two women in about their mid-thirties. One has dark-blonde curls in a messy bun. She's wearing an aggressive knee-length dress. The other seems more serious. She is tall and thin, her pale-blonde, shoulder-length hair is tightly plaited, low on the nape of her neck, she's wearing well-cut jeans and a fitted, dark T-shirt. She's calling the shots.

She seems to be the one who knows what she's doing.

The woman with the curls is pouring red wine into a large pan; in the pan are lumps of meat the size of cigarette packets. The chef is marinating cutlets in oil and herbs, and stacking them in a bowl. There's fresh mince dropping through two holes in a machine into a large tub.

Nobody is in the kitchen but the women. The digital wall clock reads 3:37.

'What d'you think?' the one with the curls asks.

'We'll be done by six,' says the other, wiping the sweat from her brow with a thin, grey towel.

BODY PARTS, WE DON'T HAVE THE DETAILS YET

The air in my fucking office is so thick, you could plait it into a ship's cable. It's hot in Hamburg. The temperature's been over thirty every day for a week. And now, this lunchtime, the city's adding a degree or two to that.

I sweep my hair out of my face and tie it up in a knot on the back of my head. I undo a few more buttons on my shirt, roll up my sleeves and turn my desk fan up from two to three. Then I drink a gulp of water, light a fresh cigarette and carry on. I'm devouring files: next week, three sex traffickers are up for trial. These guys travelled to Romania and spun village girls tales of ponies, of fantastic jobs abroad, as dancers, waitresses, au pairs. When the young women subsequently arrived in Hamburg, they were relieved of their passports and sent to work in shabby backstreet brothels in the Kiez. The scrotes carried on like this for years until we got wind of it. The usual. Somehow, no one ever notices until way too late when women or children are being abused.

Nobody ever notices in time.

I can't make up for the fact that we left the women hung out to dry for so long. But I'm going to be more prepared for this trial than I've been in my entire life. Those lousy arseholes are going to be facing the most merciless state prosecutor that a bunch of lousy arseholes has ever faced. When I'm done with them, they'll curse the day they ever got the idea of trading in people.

The women we found in a dark flat on Kastanienallee had been treated like slaves. They were all ill. The clients had been allowed to use them without condoms at thirty euros a go, and they'd all left them some nice memento or other. On top of which, four of the five women had infected wounds on their bodies and faces. And two had children, who lived in this hell with them.

Sometimes, the faces of the dead follow me, but that usually stops after two or three nights. The faces of these young women have been visiting me in my dreams for six weeks now. The fear in all their eyes. Desperate. Degraded. Beaten. And the way the children stared. As if, on one hand they didn't understand any of it, but on the other, they understood everything. Was that life? That shabby, dark hole?

My phone rings. It's Brückner.

'Rothenburgsort, boss,' he says, 'we're just setting off. Coming?'

He sounds flustered. Calabretta's still on holiday and Faller's position is yet to be filled. Inspectors Brückner and Schulle are on their own. Up to their arses in stress, the entire time.

'Course I'm coming,' I say. 'What's going on?'

'Body parts,' he says, 'we don't have the details yet.'

'Where?'

'The Billwerder Bay barrier. Want a lift?'

'I'll be with you in five.'

I switch off the fan, grab my cigarettes, my lighter and my sunglasses, and walk out. I ponder phoning Calabretta. Body parts might prove a bit much. If I call him, he'll break off his holiday. If I don't call him, I'll be the senior investigating officer till he gets back.

I don't call him.

SUMMER RETREAT, ROTHENBURGSORT

Brückner's taken charge at the crime scene, he's asking the questions. I'm not so keen on talking, anyway. Schulle has disappeared off behind a police car for a moment and is clearly getting shot of his breakfast. I light a cigarette.

SOCO are still sealing off the area. They'll shoo me away in a minute. I'm loitering on a strip of grass that runs down to the water, there's a solitary mansion behind me. The house is in good condition, painted a bright yellow, the new windows gleaming in the sun. The garden's more like a small park. I didn't know there were people with money in this neck of the woods. There's another mini-mansion a little further on, smaller, not quite as grand, more delicate, like a summer retreat. But it's also had a fresh coat of white paint not too long ago. Opposite, there's a decaying old shipyard with junk piled everywhere; to my right, the tidal barrage slams into the blue sky. The thing looks a bit like a refinery, like a mini-factory. To my surprise, I find the whole effect rather beautiful. Maybe we should come out to Rothenburgsort more often. I'll have to mention it to Klatsche and Carla.

It's hot.

Lying on a quay wall about two metres from me is the black bin bag that's brought us here. I'd hoped that my cigarette smoke would mask the stink a bit. Sadly, it doesn't work. The sack must have been in the water a while and the contents have been merrily rotting away.

'Sorry, Ms Riley, we kind of have to seal this area off now. Could you go and finish your smoke over there?'

Yeah, yeah, sure, fine.

WHAT'S WRONG WITH YOU

I get a couple of uniformed colleagues to drop me off in the Speicherstadt. There was quite a kerfuffle at the crime scene, and then the divers on top of that, plus the constant heat. When you're hanging around somewhere like a spare part, you soon start to get on people's nerves. And somebody has to check on Faller.

Since he retired three months ago, Faller has always sat in the exact same place, and he's sitting there right now – at the foot of the lighthouse. The lighthouse is in the port, at the tip of a little spit of land. Faller says that he sits there, from dawn to dusk, for fun. I don't believe a word of it. Faller's never liked sitting around anywhere.

Calabretta says that Faller sits there because he's trying to clear his head of the last thirty years, and I think he's on to something: the old man has got to sit there. Otherwise, he'd be pottering comfortably around at home, reading the paper in peace and watching the things in his garden grow. The stuff you do when you've taken early retirement, when you're sick and tired of it all.

I turn left, past the Kaispeicher. You can see the little red-and-white-ringed lighthouse from miles off. It always seems like it's made of Lego, sitting there so small and cute and so utterly pointless, looking over the massive port basin, all the container ships, cranes and huge brick buildings. Nobody actually has any use for it, apart from Faller of course; it's quite clear that *he* needs it.

The path to the lighthouse isn't paved, and the heat's made it dusty. Good job I've got boots on. I feel like Clint Eastwood in person.

Two weeks ago, when it poured for days on end, this was an ugly swamp. And I felt the same way then – like Eastwood, that is, not like a swamp.

Faller's sitting on a folding chair, he's wearing a white shirt and grey suit trousers. He's hung the jacket over the back of the chair and he's swapped his old fedora for a straw hat, to keep the sun off.

There's a fishing rod in his hand.

That's new.

'Faller?'

He turns his head, looks at me and pushes his hat up with his index finger, just a few centimetres.

'What's all this fishing-rod shit about?' I ask.

He looks back at the water.

'You're surely not going to tell me you catch any fish here, old man.'

He leans back in his seat and sighs.

'And what if you do catch anything?' I ask. 'Where are you going to put it? I can't see a bucket or anything.'

Faller looks at the water.

'Want me to get you a bit of bait, at least?'

He looks at me as if I'd asked him if he wants me to get him some coked-up teenage whores, at least.

'That was a serious question,' I say, 'you're not going to get much for supper like this.'

He stretches out his hand, I sit down beside him on the dusty ground and he puts his arm around my shoulders. My God, it's hot here, why the hell hasn't Faller got heat-stroke hours ago? A paddle steamer goes past beneath our noses. It makes me think of Belhaven in the Deep South, my dad's home town.

'Everything here is just as it should be,' says Faller.

'Why don't I believe that?'

Instead of answering, he pulls two Roth-Händles out of his shirt's breast pocket. The pocket covers the exact spot where the bullet went in. He got seriously lucky. Sometimes, I wake up in the morning with the feeling that he's not here. That his heart didn't actually make it. At those times, I try not to call him – I don't want to bother him with his own death first thing in the morning.

He pops both the cigarettes in his mouth, pulls a lighter from his trouser pocket, lights them, hands me one and says: 'You ought to get back to smoking more.'

I drag on the Roth-Händle, which makes me cough.

We stare at the water for a while, smoking.

'So, my girl,' he says, 'what's up?'

'We've found a head,' I say.

'Oh.'

'And some feet and hands.'

'Double-oh. Man or woman?'

'Man,' I say.

'Just lying around?'

'No, it was all neatly packaged up in a bin bag in the Billwerder Bay. Along with a couple of heavy stones to stop the parcel from floating.'

'So why did it surface then?'

'They're dredging,' I say. 'Clearing silt. The dredger guy got a surprise when he opened the bag.'

'Bugger. How's he doing?'

'I don't think he was that fussed. He was sitting around in the police car, getting the sun on his bare belly and cracking jokes about the weather. Seems pretty robust. He says he pulled a woman out of the water a few years ago, just around the corner at the Moorfleet Dyke.'

'And how did my lads handle it?'

'OK,' I say. 'Schulle started off by throwing up behind the car.'

'Calabretta?'

'Still in Naples,' I say, 'he's not back until Sunday.'

'Aha,' he says, taking off his straw hat and wiping away the beads of sweat with the back of his hand before putting it back on again.

'Isn't it a bit hot for you here, Faller?'

'Nope.'

I don't want to tangle with him again so I shut my mouth and just wait until I'm grilled through.

'Body parts, uh-huh. What else?'

'Nothing else,' I say.

'Sure?'

'Sure.'

'Hm,' he says. 'Sometimes, I get a funny feeling that there's something wrong with you.'

Surely not, I think.

'Well, the main thing is that there's nothing wrong with *you*,' I say.

I look at him and try to find something, a clue as to what keeps him sitting out here the whole time. But this face, which I know so well, this furrowed, friendly, fatherly phiz with the big nose and the tired eyes beneath the brim of his hat, this whole affectionate package, isn't giving anything away, not for two cents.

I look back at the water, just as he's been doing this whole time, and so we stare at the spot where the Elbe widens before eventually flowing into the sea at Cuxhaven and, as a couple of gulls sail towards the afternoon sun on the horizon between the dark-red Grosse Elbstrasse and the dark-grey docks, a cargo ship pushes its way along the channel from our left, almost soundless and the size of a multistorey car park.

LOVE IN THE TIME OF OPPRESSIVE HEAT

The thing that makes summer in Hamburg so special is that night is practically out of action. It only gets properly dark for a few hours between midnight and four in the morning – that just comes as standard between May and August, you can bank on it.

And then there are evenings like this. There's something so particular about them that you truly have to keep your wits about you. Otherwise, you might quickly start to mistake this whole thing for somewhere Mediterranean, maybe even a city by the Mediterranean Sea, and then it comes as a big shock when it's raining again the next morning and the city's only Hamburg after all.

An evening like this laps around your body like warm milk, with none of the stuff that tends to make the weather here such hard work. It's half past nine.

After I saw Faller, I went back to the office to etch those victim statements onto my brain, ready for the trial. By Monday, I want to have them internalised so that I can summon them up at will. That should keep the rage on the boil.

I let Schulle and Brückner get on with the body parts for the time being. They're going through our missing-persons files and we'll meet up tomorrow morning at the police HQ.

These days, St Pauli smells not of sea air and the warm Elbe and dark corners, but of barbecue charcoal and fire-lighters and cold beer. There aren't many gardens in this part of town, so the streets stand in for them, and here, on evenings like this, the St Paulianers sit, sweating and cel-ebrating the summer and the fact that they are here in the world, on this very spot. Some of them sit outside the pubs in the official manner, on proper chairs and tables that are all duly licensed and paid for. But most people sit outside the pubs in the unofficial manner, on random armchairs that have just been carried out with nobody having paid anyone for anything. Other people just sit any old where on the pavements, outside bars and blocks of flats, and then there's nothing but barbecuing and drinking and chatting. And in these temperatures, the Elbe's always right at the tipping point, and somehow even that just fits in perfectly. Its weighty smell makes everything just a tad more humid.

I stop at a kiosk and buy another pack of cigarettes and a beer. From the street I can see my balcony; the junk-strewn thing next to it is Klatsche's. Mine isn't exactly any great shakes, the only things going on up there are a tattered pirate flag, a neglected grapevine and an old chair that's been sat into oblivion. But Klatsche's balcony is a disaster zone. If possible, it looks even more wrecked than his poor old Volvo, and that doesn't have life easy. But then again, the Volvo only has to transport regular household rubbish; the balcony is lumbered with the bulky crap. Two and a half bicycles, a headless shop mannequin, five beer crates, a greasy barbecue from the summer of 2003, a broken TV. Two months ago, on one of the first nice evenings in May, Klatsche tried to invite me to sit out on his balcony. I asked him how that was supposed to work, and – at the very last moment, when he went to open the balcony door with two bottles of beer jammed under his arm – even he noticed that it might conceivably be a bit tricky.

'Oh,' he said, 'I didn't think of that.'

I didn't say a word, just steered him out onto my own balcony and we sat there until the morning came creeping around the corner. We don't make a habit of couply stuff like sitting around in places, staring out into the night. After all, we're just two people who keep getting stuck on each other. Night owls, allies. But now and then, romance takes hold of us. Although it soon gets too much for us and we don't know what we're meant to do with it, and then it almost inevitably collapses and tastes flat, and we're left standing around like a pair of idiots. That's why we tend to prefer pub crawls and constantly resealing our friendship and going a couple of weeks without either of us stumbling into the other person's bed. At times like that, Klatsche likes to stumble into other beds altogether, he says it happens by accident and he doesn't mean to. I'm happy to believe the didn't-mean-to part, but not the by-accident. Still, I try not to take it personally.

I unlock the street door, head up the stairs to the third floor where, instead of opening my front door, I knock on his. It takes a while, but eventually I hear shuffling, then a yawn, then the door opens. Klatsche's wearing bright-blue boxers and a dark-green T-shirt that's too small and a bit shabby round the neck. The fag in his hand must have gone out some time ago. He looks like a bandit.

'Hey, Madam Prosecutor.'

'Hey,' I say. 'What're you up to?'

'I'm lying in front of the open fridge.'

'Mind if I join you?' I ask.

'Sure, I'm not going to let my girl peg out in this heat.'

He pulls me through the door and drops a kiss on the top of my head.

'I'm not your girl,' I say.

'I know, baby, I know.'

I DON'T WANT TO BE ANYWHERE HIPSTER COUPLES GO

Brückner and Schulle look like they've just come in from the playground. One's wearing a thin T-shirt and the other's got his threadbare Liverpool shirt on, they both have uncombed hair kind of pushed out of their faces – Brückner's goes more back, while Schulle's goes more up – and the bright, northern-European sun is shining out of their faces. Like they've been on holiday to Seacrow Island. I've really grown to like these two, the way I used to like the boys in the back row at school.

'*Moin*, boss,' says Schulle, raising a hand; Brückner grins and picks his nose, probably without even noticing.

I often wonder what these guys would do with themselves if they had to wear uniform.

'*Moin*, gentlemen,' I say. 'How's business?'

'Tidy,' says Brückner. 'We know who we pulled out of the water yesterday.'

'Oh, that was quick work. Who is it?'

'Dejan Pantelic,' he says. 'Aged thirty-one, professional

musician. Came to Hamburg from Belgrade in the mid-nineties. No family left here. His girlfriend reported him missing on Monday this week.'

Pinned to the wall behind his desk are the photographs taken in pathology of the head from the Billwerder Bay. Next to them is a slightly scruffy picture of a guy in shorts and a Hawaiian shirt. He's standing beside a palm tree with a cocktail in hand and a look on his face that suggests he thinks pretty highly of his own appearance. With the best will in the world, I can't see much resemblance between him and our head.

'The same guy?' I ask. 'Are you sure?'

'He's just a bit swollen,' says Brückner. 'His girlfriend identified him this morning, without a shadow of a doubt.'

'Oh,' I say, 'that can't have been very nice.'

'Schulle did it,' he says.

'Oh,' I say again.

And Schulle says: 'Got to be done. That was my first floater, and it wasn't even in one piece. But it'll be OK.'

Brückner yawns and digs around in his nose again. There's something up there.

'So how many have *you* seen?' I ask him.

'No idea,' he says nasally. 'I trained on missing persons. We were constantly pulling people out of the water. Kind of routine. My God, the sight of them. Yesterday's was a piece of piss in comparison.'

Really.

'So, what else do we know about this, what was his name again?'

'Pantelic,' he says. 'He was last seen Friday night or the early hours of Saturday morning, in the Kiez. Went to the Silbersack with two mates, and they reckon he headed home around two. Or that's what they told his girlfriend, anyway. We haven't had a word with the mates yet, but I will in a bit.'

'OK,' I say. 'What else have we got?'

'The divers didn't find a thing,' says Schulle, packing up his stuff. 'The Elbe is somewhat less than crystal in this heat. SOCO found plenty of fag ends and hairs and tyre tracks in the grass where they dredged him up, but they won't get us very far. The whole Billwerder Bay is kind of a hang-out for hipster couples at the weekend.'

Damn. OK, maybe we won't be heading out to Rothenburgsort more often then. I don't want to be anywhere hipster couples go.

'OK,' I say, 'so you two are going to have a chat to our body's mates then?'

'Brückner can do that,' says Schulle. 'I want to pop round to the Thousand Bollocks – one or two of the residents there might have seen something.'

'Can I tag along?' I ask.

'Sure,' says Schulle.

I'm a big fan of the House of the Thousand Bollocks. It's a tower block in Rothenburgsort and kind of the first port of call for ex-cons. They move in there when they get out of jail – five or six guys crammed into one tiny flat. The Thousand Bollocks is kind of a pressure cooker for criminals – rammed full of despair, frustration and testosterone. It's all male in there, and the place regularly explodes. It makes total sense to ask around there, seeing that people are being found chopped up in that neck of the woods.

Brückner presses his index finger against his left nostril and sniffs so loudly that somebody's going to have to say something.

'Something up with your nose?' I ask.

'Not really,' he says. 'There was this night about ten years ago when I did two lines of coke instead of just one, and anytime it gets this hot it kind of flares up.'

Oh. Right.

'It wasn't just that one night,' says Schulle. 'You were like that the whole time in those days, dickhead.'

Brückner sticks his finger up at Schulle and looks back at his computer screen.

The boys from the back row, I'm telling you.

THE HOUSE OF THE THOUSAND BOLLOCKS

At first glance, it looks like your average tower block in your average rough part of town. On the ground floor, the windows are smashed, the door is broken, the mailboxes have been firebombed and the hundred or so seventies' name plates are hidden deep beneath several layers of graffiti. But by the time you reach the stairs, you can see that this place is in another league, there's a circle of five shaggy guys smoking crack. They pay us no attention. The right-hand lift is broken, there's a sleeping bag that used to be green or blue in the corner of the left-hand one. Leaking into the sleeping bag is an open tin of ravioli, next to it, there's a cardboard crate of Hansa Pils. It reeks of discount booze.

Schulle presses the button marked nine.

'Who are we visiting?' I ask.

'Grandpa Terim,' he says, 'he's lived here for decades – if two of the cockroaches were to get married, he'd be able to tell you all about it. He makes this place work. Besides, he's so old that no one can touch him now.'

'So he'll talk to us?'

'If he's in the mood,' says Schulle. 'And we're not coming empty-handed, which won't hurt.'

'Aren't we?' I ask.

He pulls a little baggie of top-grade skunk from his trouser pocket and holds it under my nose.

'Drugs squad,' he says, 'I've got a friend who—'

I really don't want to know.

'I really don't want to know,' I say.

The lift doors open. The building is U-shaped and on every floor there's a kind of concrete walkway, and each flat – or, to be more precise, each shared cell – opens off it. At least ten per floor. Schulle marches through to the back left. There's no handle on the door. Hanging over the doorframe is a clearly ancient Bob Marley poster. Inspector Schulle knocks. *Tap. Tap. Tap, tap, tap.* Two long, three short.

'Look at you, smart guy,' I say.

He grins at me.

Someone inside calls out: '*Merhaba*!'

'*Merhaba*,' says Schulle, giving the door a gentle kick; it swings cautiously open.

Beyond the door is a stoner den, straight out of the stoner den textbook, although it must once have been a one-room flat. There are mouldy tie-dye cloths covering the windows, the walls are caked with a thick layer of yellow, there's some kind of kickboxing show on the telly but nobody's watching it. There's little furniture. At the front, there's a space the size estate agents count as half a room, probably FKA the kitchen; it's full of rubbish. In the back of the room, there's a tatty couch. The guy on the couch must be Grandpa Terim. Grandpa Terim has lost his legs. The stumps of his thighs are wrapped in something green, black and yellow, I'm guessing Jamaican flags. Even with legs, Grandpa Terim probably wouldn't have been very tall; without legs, he's tiny. A tiny scrap of legless gangster. His grey beard is wispy, on his head there's a greasy black leather cap, on his face are outsized aviator sunglasses. If you take into account the dim light weaving its way through the gaff, there's no way he can see a thing.

He gives us a friendly smile.

Schulle leans against the wall to the right of the couch, I follow suit. Grandpa Terim turns his head in our direction. I'm really not sure if he can see us.

'So?'

His voice sounds like very fine sandpaper. Thin and scratchy.

'We've brought you something,' says Schulle. He gives him the packet of weed.

'Thanks,' he scratches, 'thank you, thank you…'

He nods about twenty times and starts rolling a joint on the spot.

'What do you two want?'

'Anyone lost their shit around here lately?' asks Schulle.

'Someone loses their shit around here every day. They're all bonkers,' says Grandpa Terim, distributing a spectacular helping of weed onto his tobacco.

Schulle says nothing but ostentatiously checks the fit of his pistol in its holster. I try not to stare too hard at Grandpa Terim's leg stumps. Somehow, it always freaks me out when people have had things amputated.

The joint's ready and the old man starts smoking. The thing's so fat that just watching is making my fuses glow. Schulle and I breathe as little as we can and seeing that he's keeping his trap shut, I do too – Schulle's the one in charge here, no question.

'No, seriously,' says Grandpa Terim, taking a deep drag and leaning back. His stumps tilt upward slightly. He blows out the smoke. 'Everything here's the same as ever.'

'New neighbours, maybe?' asks Schulle.

Grandpa Terim spreads his arms wide and lays them along the backrest. A bit of ash drops off his spliff and burns a hole in his sofa.

'Yeah,' he says, 'good handful. Get a few fresh out of jail every week.'

Schulle raises his eyebrows.

'All small fry,' says Grandpa Terim. 'Poor sods.'

He drags on his spliff. More ash drops off, this time it lands on his right stump. It doesn't seem to bother him.

'They're not in your league, my friend,' he says. 'You lot are after bigger fish, aren't you.'

He releases the smoke again and interlinks his hands behind his head. There's an ember dancing on his cap.

'This place is very chill right now. Might be the calmest in this whole pissing part of town.'

Seems to me like he might be right there. On our drive over, I was thinking that the people around here are getting poorer and poorer and, as they do, they get more and more aggressive. The mere sight of society's weeping sores is painful. Rich Hamburg is doing better year after year, quaffing champers twenty-four-seven. Poor Hamburg is doing shittier day after day, it's twenty-four-seven despair. My city is basically a sociological disaster zone. There's this one S-Bahn line that makes me twitchy every time. You get on at the Jungfernstieg, next to the Alster, where Hamburg has more shitting luxury than it knows what to do with. And three stops later, on the Veddel, there are children with rings under their eyes, feeding themselves on stale, cheapo sliced white while their parents drink away the dole. And nothing about that has changed for years – in the city with the most millionaires in all of Germany.

'So you're sure we're barking up the wrong tree here?' asks Schulle.

'If you weren't,' says Grandpa Terim, 'I'd tell you. You know that.'

'Yeah, I know,' says Schulle.

He looks at me.

'C'mon, we're out of here,' he says.

'That's it?' I ask.

'Yeah. If Gramps here says there's nothing doing, there's nothing doing.'

My gut tells me that Schulle's right. The bodies in the Elbe and the bodies in these flats have nothing whatever to do with each other.

My phone rings. It's Klatsche.

'Where are you?' he asks.

'At the House of the Thousand Bollocks,' I say, dripping with self-importance. Klatsche appreciates that kind of gag and I want to make him laugh.

But he doesn't laugh.

'You have to come home,' he says. His voice sounds like he's sitting in a cellar, eating rocks.

I have to hold on to Schulle for a moment.

'What's up?' I ask.

'I'm not sure,' he says. 'But whatever it is, it's up with Carla.'

BUY SCUM, GET SCUM FREE

'She won't tell me what happened,' Klatsche says as he opens the door to me. 'And I'm not allowed to touch her. I found her clinging to the front steps just now, in a total state. I barely managed to scrape her up.'

He gives his stubbly chin a dishevelled rub.

I give him a quick peck on the cheek and push him out of the way.

'Where is she?'

'Living room.'

I walk into the living room.

There are moments that deserve more cigarettes than a person can stand. They deserve to be blacked out and blasted with nerve poison, sunk forever in the fog. My hands are shaking as I light up.

Carla, my friend and companion, my mother and my daughter all rolled into one, my goddamn family, is cowering in a corner of Klatsche's living room. She's drawn up her legs and is gripping them tightly, her face is buried in her chest and over it all lie her dark curls, as listless as an old blanket. She's rocking forward and back, forward and back, forward and back. Her arms and legs are covered with dust, scratches and bruises. She looks like she's been dragged across the Reeperbahn. I drag on my cigarette, then kneel in front of her and lay my hands on her shoulders. She flinches.

'It's me,' I say quietly, 'it's only me.'

She keeps rocking.

'Carla,' I say, 'look at me.'

Forward, back, forward, back.

'Carla? Can you hear me?'

No reaction.

I squeeze her a little tighter.

Mistake.

She hits my hands away and kicks out, I fly back and crash onto the floorboards. I burn my hand in the attempt to keep hold of my cigarette.

Carla looks at me.

Her left eye is almost completely swollen shut, her lips are split, there's dried blood under her nose.

I pick myself off the floor, throw the cigarette out of the window and sit back down beside Carla.

I try to take her hands. That works now, and I hold them tight with one hand while very cautiously stroking her hair with the other.

She's still looking at me.

The rocking has stopped.

'Carla, what happened?'

The tears start to flow from her intact eye.

'Was it a man?'

She shakes her head and buries it again.

Then she says something.

'What?' I whisper.

She says it again.

And then I understand.

Two, she says.

It was two men.

NEVER HAPPENING AGAIN

So, these two bastards just came along and raped her, for almost the whole night, down in the cellar, at her own place. Now she's sleeping, has been for almost six hours.

It's Wednesday evening, eight o'clock, she's lying on my sofa, I'm sitting next to her, holding her hand. I don't know exactly what happened last night, I only hope I can get her to go to the police quickly. I've already told the guys on the sex-crimes squad and they'll get to work on Carla's cellar. But unless she makes a statement, there really isn't anything much they can do.

I stand up, pull the curtains aside and let the evening in. It's still easily twenty-four degrees. Outside, legions of flip-flops and wooden clogs are slapping and clattering over the cobblestones, a bottle of beer is opened every ten seconds, and the birds are singing their little brains out. A very old song tinkles out a few windows along. Everything is as lovely as ever, soft and colourful and scruffy, but it's all just a pile of shit.

THAT CAN GO WRONG TOO, YOU KNOW

I'm standing by the open living-room window, drinking coffee. It's just after six, the sky is very bright blue and the wobbly old antennae on the rooftops opposite stretch themselves towards it like thin little arms. The sun's already here, laying a soft shimmer over the roofs. It'll be about an hour before it explodes, but then it'll be full force until the evening. I take a deep breath. Normally, the north-German air hisses in your throat a little in the mornings, because it's always a touch cooler than you expect. But this morning, when it's easily over twenty, it slips right down.

Carla is lying on the sofa, sleeping, has been for over sixteen hours now. Although the water bottle I put there for her is empty.

'Let her just sleep, as long as she wants to,' Klatsche said. 'Carla has good instincts. She knows best what she needs.'

I go over to her, cautiously stroke her hair, walk to the bedroom and crawl back into the warm bed with Klatsche, to warm my cold heart. He grumbles a little, flops over to me and his upper body almost covers me up. I look at him.

Once the burglar king, the man with the best locksmith service in town, the boy who still roams the Kiez day and night, just the way he always did. He doesn't pull any jobs these days, keeps as far out of the underworld as possible, but even so, he's never really left it. Maybe that's why I'm so attached to him. He's my link to a world that draws me to it the way the devil's drawn to the fire and brimstone, but which I can never really enter. I'm not the only one who suspects that if I did, I'd change sides. Faller always said that very thing. That I'm really a crook with a gangster brain.

For whatever reason.

Klatsche's bristly dark-blond hair, his strong brow, his high cheekbones, his perilously curved lips, the freckles on his nose. There are a few lines crinkling around his eyes. Too long looking into the sun.

I cling tighter to him.

LET THE PROFESSIONALS GET ON WITH THEIR WORK

She was still asleep when I did eventually leave the flat.

'She's been sleeping for almost twenty hours,' Klatsche had said.

'For nineteen hours and fifteen minutes to be precise.'

'What?'

'Nothing.'

Now I'm sitting at the State Prosecution Service, leafing through the files for the human-trafficking trial. Calabretta did some real good work there, it's all watertight, I can't wait to see what the guys' lawyers try to build their defence on. When I look at this, all they can really do is nod and say: Right-oh, then, we'll take seven to eight years inside, thank you very much, bye.

I make a few notes in the margin, bring the desk fan closer to my face and wonder if I should chase up the sex-crimes team. I know that there's not much they can do without a statement from Carla, but they ought to have combed through her cellar by now. Maybe something's turned up that they can get going on.

I wonder what Faller would do – he'd most likely not call. Let the professionals get on with their work is what he always says. Which is true, of course. What good would it do if I phoned? I light a cigarette. It tastes kind of bitter.

EASILY PUSHING NINETY

It's around fourish when the statements and investigation details melt together into a lumpy mass in my brain. My colleagues have all knocked off for the day, there's not a soul around. I exhale, shut the files, lock them away and set off for Faller.

I'm in the mood for old, frustrated ex-copper.

When I reach the Speicherstadt, the heat settles on my head like a helmet, the massive redbrick warehouses have turned the narrow lanes and canals into a giant oven and my boots stick to the tarmac joins between the cobblestones. No wind, not anywhere. This doesn't happen here. It's always cool in the Speicherstadt. That's what it was damn well built for.

On the radio just now, they said there'll be a new record temperature set this afternoon, eighty-six degrees C, I think they said, can't remember exactly. At the moment I'd say we're easily pushing ninety. There's nobody about.

Hanseatic Hamburg, now also available in spaghetti western.

I call Klatsche.

'Carla was awake for five minutes just now,' he says. 'Drank a bottle of water. Now she's gone back to sleep.'

I stop, slip a cigarette into my mouth and feel my boots sinking into the tar.

'Did she say anything?'

'Rough play,' he says.

'What?'

'She said "rough play".'

'And nothing else?'

'Nothing else,' he says. 'And then she turned over and went straight back to sleep.'

'Thank you for looking after her.'

'No worries. Where are you?'

'Going to see Faller,' I say.

'OK. Say hi from me.'

I throw my cigarette away. I never thought I'd say this, but it's just too hot to smoke.

THAT FUCKING ROD

Faller's not alone. There's a young man in uniform facing him and they're talking. He's an enforcement officer from the public-order department. To the best of my knowledge, my former colleague has no fishing licence. So Faller has clearly been caught poaching.

Even from a distance, I can see that both men, the young and the old alike, are sweating buckets. The old man raises his hands to the heavens in gratitude as he sees me coming.

'Chas, will you please tell him that I don't need a fishing licence.'

'Mr Faller doesn't need a fishing licence,' I say, even though I have no idea how that could possibly be true.

'Uh-huh,' says the man from the public-order office as he looks at me. He's got a weirdly thin voice. Sounds like some little Nazi henchman in a trashy Hollywood film.

'And why would that be, may I ask? Because he's actually Zorro?'

'He's not Zorro,' I say. Although I'm slowly starting to

suspect that Faller considers himself to be something of that sort.

The man in uniform is getting impatient but doesn't say so yet, just raises his eyebrows unpleasantly.

'I'm a retired police officer,' says Faller.

'SO WHAT?'

OK, now he's blown it.

'Yes,' says Faller, 'and retired police officers don't need fishing licences.'

I think he sounds a touch patronising.

'WHERE DOES IT SAY THAT THEN?'

'Nowhere,' says Faller. 'That's just how it is.'

'Ha,' says the public-order office man, 'as if.'

The two of them are facing each other in the sweltering heat of the Kaispeicher. One in a white shirt and straw hat, the other in a dark-blue shirt and uniform cap; large damp patches are spreading across both their shirts. I stand so that I can pull the two of them apart at any time, should this turn into a bar-room brawl. Although the stress in the air is definitely not emanating from Faller. He looks like he's got a resting pulse of below sixty.

'That's enough fooling around,' says the man from the public-order office. 'Hand over the rod and your ID, and there'll be a hefty fine to pay, Mr Retired Police Officer.'

'Nah,' says Faller.

He turns away, sits back down on his little chair, lights a Roth-Händle, picks up his fishing rod and sighs contentedly. I'll eat my hat if he opens his mouth again in the presence of the public-order guy.

'That's it, I've had it, I'll be back tomorrow. And if you're still sitting here and fishing, I'm getting the police involved.'

Faller just pulls his hat a fraction further down over his face.

I tell the man from the office that he's welcome to do that, to get the police involved. But that he shouldn't count on our colleagues there bothering their colleague here. Not over a fishing licence. He shakes his head and flounces off.

Faller blinks at the water and grins.

I sit next to him. And when I see him grinning like that, it hits me anew how much it stinks no longer having him at my side every day.

'What's happened?' he asks.

'Why do you ask?'

'Don't take me for a mug, Chas.'

I light a cigarette and take a deep breath.

'Carla was raped. By two guys. She's in a shit way.'

Faller heaves himself out of his chair, sits down beside me on the dusty ground and takes me in his arms.

I instantly lose my self-control, start blubbing. And now I've started, I can't stop. The tears pour out of me like I've got a watering can in my head. Chastity Riley, formidable public prosecutor and unstoppable crying machine. Feared for her floods of tears. Faller holds me tight and strokes my hair.

'There are times,' he says, 'when our lives throw up even more shit than our jobs.'

Right, I think – all of a sudden, there are body parts floating in the Elbe and my only female friend has been brutally raped and is in a comatose sleep, which is a bit like she's dead.

I pull away, stand up, wipe my face and clap the dust off my trousers. Kindly meant, Faller, but don't make me fucking well cry ever again.

'And what exactly is up with you, old man?'

He leans back a bit and looks at me as if a ship just sprouted out of my head.

'Why are you cluttering the place up with all your pointless fishing?'

He stands up and sits back in his chair.

'What the fuck is this? Why did you leave the police? Why did you walk out on me? So that you could mess with the public-order office at your leisure? If you want trouble, there are far easier ways of getting it!'

I'm flustered. I don't often get flustered.

'Your nose is running,' he says.

'No,' I say.

'Yes,' he says.

He reaches into his shirt pocket, pulls out a fresh cotton handkerchief and holds it out to me. It's been ironed. I take it and blow my nose.

'I'll wash it and bring it back some day.'

He nods, puts his hat back on, takes his rod and throws out the line.

That fucking rod.

Intriguing. I'm jealous of a fishing rod.

'This is such stupid shit,' I say, making tracks. Faller's still speaking, but I'm not listening anymore.

Dark clouds are gathering when I get to the landing bridges. As I pass the Millerntor stadium, the storm is gearing up. Just before I get home, it thunders. As I sit next to Klatsche with Carla, there's a flash of lightning and then it thunders right over our heads, and then the first fat raindrops fall.

At that very moment, Carla wakes up.

She stretches, she sits up, she pulls her legs up to her body, she strokes her hair out of her face. The swelling around her eye has gone down a bit, there's an extensive shiner there now, her lips and nose are scabby.

'Hey,' says Klatsche, 'sleepyhead.'

Carla looks at us.

Her expression is as dark as the sky and she says: 'Can I have a beer and a cigarette please?'

It's raining giants out there, in no time at all there's a new population plummeting to earth, and because none of us gets up to shut the window, it doesn't take a minute before there's water in my living room. Sometimes, the weather's so in sync with life that I could puke.

You have to kill a pig of this sort quickly. If you leave time for the adrenaline to flow, the meat will taste bitter. To prevent anything spoiling, remove the innards speedily, chop them finely and discard. Before rigor mortis sets in, hang the body by the feet and let it bleed out. Ideally, catch the blood in a large tub. Too much protein will block the drip tray in the drain, which is unpleasant, and this way, you can make black pudding too. Debone the extremities and pass the meat through the mincer, cut the long bones to size with the bone saw and cook them up. The resulting stock is sure to come in handy.

Split the rump in two and hang for a good half hour.

Take the tenderloins, breast and belly off the bone and marinate in red wine.

Rub the saddle chops with olive oil and herbs.

The mince is perfect for sausages, e.g. bratwurst or salsiccia. Season with mace, allspice, rosemary, chilli, salt and black pepper.

The wine-marinated tenderloins make a lovely ragout when braised with tomatoes.

The saddle chops are best grilled or pan fried.

HEARD THE MICHEL STRIKE THE HOUR

We're at HQ, sitting in a colleague's office. The woman from the sex-crimes squad is good, objective and careful, she doesn't tug at Carla. I'm staying in the background, by the window, trying to keep a low profile. There was probably no need for me to have come at all. Carla seems so incredibly poised. She talks about the rape as if she's rattling off a recipe for potato salad:

She'd just shut her café, shortly after eight, and had gone back into the kitchen to do the accounts, like she does every evening. She was counting her money when suddenly, there were two guys standing in the doorway. One was tall and strong, thirty to thirty-five years old, short, dark-blond hair, square jaw, acne scars, checked shirt, black jeans, bulbous nose, thin lips. The other was more on the small and wiry side, forty to forty-five years old. He had slightly longer, reddish-blond hair and a stubbly beard, he was wearing a green T-shirt, pale trousers, noticeably smeary glasses, and he had a squint in his right eye. Both of them had been sitting at the bar an hour earlier, but at some point, they'd vanished. Carla had assumed that they'd skipped out without paying while she'd been in the kitchen. But they hadn't done a runner, they'd locked themselves in the loos.

They dragged her into the cellar. And while one of them held a broken wine bottle to her throat, the other laid into her. They took turns, again and again, it went on until just before midnight. Carla heard the Michel strike the hour when they finally left. They'd raped her seven times in total.

'I can't remember what happened after that,' she says.

She's sitting bolt upright on the very edge of the chair, her legs crossed. She's sitting there as taut as a bowstring, she could jump up and run at any moment. She scorns the tissues the policewoman put out for her.

'You can't remember how you got out of the cellar?'

'On all fours, I guess,' says Carla.

The officer sticks her pencil into her bun.

'What now?' Carla asks. 'Do we do identikits?'

My colleague nods. As the two of them leave the office together, Carla glances at me. All the shine's gone out of her eyes, she looks like a zombie.

'Carla,' I say, 'I need to pop in to see Brückner and Schulle. Will you call me when you're finished here? So I can take you home?'

She doesn't reply.

'I'll let you know,' says the policewoman.

BY THE ELBOW

Brückner and Schulle are coming towards me down the corridor, on the double. Even before I can ask what's up, Brückner says: 'Another parcel, boss, also in Billwerder Bay.'

'Coming?' Schulle asks, but he's already steering me along by the elbow.

'Sure,' I say.

We're heading towards the underground car park; I pull out my phone and call Carla. She doesn't answer. I try the switchboard and get put through to the inspector who took Carla's statement.

'Your friend has already left. She asked me not to call you.'

'Uh-huh,' I say.

'I got the impression that she wanted to be alone,' she says.

OK, Carla, so that's how it is.

But playing the lone wolf is kind of more my job.

MEH

The dredger operator is really proud of his find, but who wouldn't be – after all, it's the second exciting parcel he's pulled out of the water in the space of three days. He's leaning against the police car, next to one of the pair of uniformed officers, and grinning, his ol' fancy-dress sea captain's cap stuck on his rather sweaty head and his bare belly glinting in the sun.

Schulle parks the car and looks charily at me and Brückner. He can't face the parcel. I can't face the belly.

'You take the dredger guy, we'll take the floater?' I ask.

'Thanks,' he says.

'*Da nich für*,' says Brückner – don't mention it.

We get out.

The sun burns the top of my head.

There's a uniformed policewoman standing on the quay wall, guarding the mud-encrusted packet. Brückner drops to his knees and takes a slightly closer look at the thing without touching it. I stay a little way off to the side and wonder whether anything's catching my eye, whether anything here is different from Tuesday. Whether anyone else has been here, for example. The guys with all the SOCO shit were intending to come straight here from another crime scene, but now they're stuck in traffic in the Elbtunnel. Please. Who drives through the Elbtunnel. The policewoman comes over to me, we nod to each other, I light a cigarette.

'Want one?'

'Thanks,' she says, 'but I'm trying to give up.'

'Oh,' I say. 'How's it going?'

'It's hell.'

All of us but Schulle, who's busy with the chunky witness, are standing around like lemons because we're waiting for the SOCO equipment and its associated experts.

'It's a very neatly packed parcel,' says the policewoman, 'don't you think?'

'I was just thinking that myself,' I say, 'stands out a mile, doesn't it?'

'That's how my mum packs parcels,' she says.

I have no idea how my mother packs parcels, but I tend to agree that this one here was not packed by a man. The sides of the black bin bag are meticulously folded over and the parcel tape is stuck at precise right angles. I didn't spot that with the first parcel, but hey, Mr Dredger Operator had had his fingers all over it by then.

'It's strange,' says the policewoman. 'I can't imagine a woman doing a thing like that, dismembering someone.'

'Maybe there's a couple involved,' I say.

'A woman and her charming assistant?'

She grins cheekily to herself as she says that, and I find myself smiling slightly too.

Weird, in the circumstances.

I mean, this kind of thing normally makes me pass out – dismemberment, mutilation and chopped-up bodies are not exactly up my street. This shit normally gets me kind of down. But somehow, none of it really seems to affect me this time. The policewoman apparently feels much the same. As if we didn't give a damn what's in the parcel. With the best will in the world, I can't explain why that should be.

Aha, SOCO have made it through the tunnel but they haven't quite got this far yet – they're over there, sealing everything and everybody off. That's nice of them, I could just do with being sealed off right now.

Schulle's still occupied with the dredger guy, while Brückner and I are waiting for the SOCO team to set about the parcel with a scalpel. Hollerieth, their boss, is here in person, taking charge and is, as ever, grouchiness incarnate. If he'd just *once* say what it is that pisses him off so much, I'd at least know whether or not to actually feel guilty anytime he's around.

'Here we go then,' he says, slitting open the black bin bag, while giving us a look as if we haven't wiped the blackboard.

First I see one foot, then the other, then a hand and then a face. Moustache, short ash-blond hair, sloping forehead, longish head. There's suddenly this phrase rattling nonstop round my head. God knows where it sprang from. It's not nice: *Meh, one less ugly bloke in the world.*

'Boss?' Brückner taps me on the upper arm with his finger.

'Er, yeah?' I say, 'what was that?'

He was clearly saying something, but I didn't hear. He says it again.

'I'll call the divers out, OK?'

'Sure,' I say, 'the divers, yes, of course.'

I rub my eyes and come back to earth.

'Get them to dig out this entire basin, as far downriver as the timber port. I don't want the dredger guy to find yet another parcel tomorrow. Otherwise, he'll be turning up at HQ wanting a job.'

'Oh Lord,' says Brückner, looking over my shoulder.

I turn and then I see it too. Moving in behind us, all squealing tyres and blue flashing lights on their heads, are the press.

MY HUSBAND DRANK SO MUCH

It's Saturday and, as so often at the weekend, I have absolutely no idea what to do with myself. If I didn't have my work in the week, I'd be long dead. Normally, I go down to see Carla in her café and hang around there for a bit, but Carla's café is shut. Because Carla's shut, or something very like shut. Klatsche's not here either. He drove Carla to the seaside very early this morning, to take her mind off things. I could have gone along too of course, it's forecast to be another hot day today, but I'm waiting for phone calls. Brückner and Schulle were out and about yesterday, turning Dejan Pantelic's circles upside down. And the divers have been back scouring Billwerder Bay since dawn. If they find anything, I want to be on the spot ASAP.

There are baby clothes hanging up in the window opposite. Tiny dresses and jumpers, knitted in all the gaudy colours of the sweetshop. Living in the flat is an old woman with a grey perm, she lives alone there and she knits the stuff. She then hangs her latest wares up on her curtain pole, but only the Hamburg sky knows who it's for. She herself sits behind the curtain. Sometimes she cries. She thinks you can't see.

'My husband drank so much,' she told me once.

It was only then that I realised she'd been widowed a few months earlier. I'd thought she'd always been alone.

Of course, I could go and check on Faller.

SUMMER FOOTBALL

Faller's brought a parasol with him. That's a good thing in my opinion, because it means he clearly *is* still thinking for himself. In other respects, the situation is unchanged. Sits there wearing a straw hat, fishing.

'I brought us some fish rolls and cigarettes,' I say.

'Are the fish rolls cold?'

'Of course.'

I hold one of the rolls out to him.

'Ah,' he says. 'Bismarck herring.'

I sit beside him on the wall. We eat. I wait till he's finished then I tell him what we found.

'Fancy that,' he says, pulling in the line and throwing it back out.

'Is that all you can think of?'

'Yup,' he says.

'Aren't you interested in what's going on?'

'Nope,' he says, 'not one bit.'

'That strikes me as strange,' I say.

'Doesn't me,' he says.

End of conversation.

I pull the cigarettes out of my pocket, light two and give him one. We smoke. The line doesn't move.

'Did the dude from the public-order office turn up again?' I ask.

'Hasn't shown his face.'

The pale-brown sunshade that Faller's put up is big enough to cast a muddy shadow over us both. It's like we're sitting in a circle that links the port and the sky, and we'll take in a couple of gulls too. For the first time, it occurs to me that my old friend here might be doing the exact right thing. Maybe everything is perfectly fine like this, stepping on the brake and stopping the wheels for a moment when life's been going too fast. Pressing pause. My only mistake was thinking that he'd already done that when he retired. He needed to retire. He almost kicked the bucket on our last mission. And he's never shaken off the business a couple of years ago, the time Chief Inspector Faller ventured too far out into the swamp. Sitting here now, fishing and staring at the water, and doing so until his soul's had time to heal from the last thirty years, probably *is* the best thing he could be doing. And the lighthouse is a good spot for that kind of thing. Near a lighthouse, there's always light.

'You know what, Faller,' I say, 'as far as I'm concerned, you can sit here for all eternity if it does you good.'

I drag on my cigarette.

'It is doing you good, right?'

He nods, takes off his hat and wipes his head with a handkerchief. It's a long time since I saw him without a hat. His hair's always been a shade of grey. For as long as I've known him. Of course the shade has changed over the years, but it was always grey. Now it's white. I'm not sure if that makes him look cuddly or wise or just old and knackered.

'It's like this,' he says, 'the little fish travel in a shoal, in a group. They do that so that they can look out for each other. Because when there's a lot of you, you can defend yourselves better, and it's not so easy to swim in the wrong direction.'

He flaps his hat around in front of his face, probably with the aim of cooling off.

'Other fish, predators, swim alone.'

He puts his hat back on his head, pulls in the line and throws it back out again.

'And then,' he says, 'there are fish who spun out at a corner, who lost their shoal. They can't remember exactly where they're meant to be going. And so as not to accidentally cross paths with a predator, they find some safe place and wait in peace. They wait until their shoal happens to pass by again. Or another shoal that they can join. Or they wait for something else, but even they don't know what it is.'

The spoon lure bobs in the water at our feet.

'Be nice if the football was on this evening,' I say.

'Yes,' he says, 'that would be nice.'

But sadly, the Bundesliga is taking a break just now, because anything Faller can do, they've been able to do for ages.

BOSSA NOVA

I took the first ferry that came to hand. I was a bit wobbly after Faller's fable. I don't know who it was about. Whether he meant him or me, or if he's just going soft in the head. In any case, I suddenly wasn't so steady on my pins. And in cases like this, it always helps just to give up on solid ground beneath your feet and to swap it for a few ship planks. When the subsurface is moving, you're less likely to notice your own instability.

I'm sitting on the thin wooden bench in the bow, the little launch is ploughing through the port basin, sitting next to me is a punk. He's still very young, but he's the real thing. Not just a fashion punkanista like you get these days. He smells of beer and black tobacco, he's crazily thin and his trousers are so dirty they could stand up by themselves. There are holes in his Doc Martens and he's lost his front tooth, probably not too long ago. The punk looks battered, but he seems in a good mood. It's afternoon and the sun is gradually taking on a motherly hue. We cruise along the Hafenstrasse and St Pauli glitters brightly. The captain's playing music, some kind of bossa nova. Everything's swaying to the beat.

The punk lets a sigh fall over the railing, and I see a tear on his face, but I also see the smile, and then he says: 'My God, this city's beautiful.'

I need to get us two beers on the spot.

SARK YOU

Hallelujah, she's eating again. She spent two days just sleeping, then another two days just drinking beer and smoking cigarettes, but now she's sitting with me on some front steps in the sun, dunking a croissant into her coffee.

She almost looks back to normal.

The shiner around her left eye is still shimmering in shades of purple and green, but it's paler now. The wounds on her face are healing. Her dark-brown hair is washed and glossy. But she's not wearing a dress. She's borrowed a T-shirt from Klatsche, some music thing, some band – there are dates on the back, from some tour back in 1998. The jeans are mine, they're way too long for her, she's had to turn them up a couple of times.

'I'll buy myself a few pairs of trousers tomorrow,' she says, chewing. 'You feel much quicker in trousers.'

She takes a sip of coffee.

'That's why you always wear trousers, right?'

'Beats me,' I say, 'maybe. I've never worn anything else.'

'I'll get another of these croissants,' she says, standing up and clapping the dust off her legs. 'Want one?'

'No,' I say, 'thank you,' and watch as she cautiously looks left and right before crossing the road, and as she only opens the door to the Kandie Shop a crack and slips in quickly, as if she feels watched by somebody. And she doesn't waggle her bum once, the whole time. Somehow, her frivolity has gone.

Those fucking wankers.

I put my sunglasses on and light a cigarette. It feels like it's already nearly thirty degrees. It's not even noon.

'Hey,' says Klatsche.

He's suddenly standing in front of me.

'Hey,' I say.

He bends down and gives me a kiss on the forehead.

'Where's Carla?'

'Getting herself a croissant,' I say.

'To eat?'

'No, to play chess with.'

'What's making you so sarky?'

I don't know.

'Sorry,' I say.

He shrugs, climbs onto the step behind me, drops down and takes a seat. I hand a cigarette and my coffee to him over my shoulder.

'Thanks, baby,' he says. And adds, an octave higher: 'Don't call me baby!'

Oh man. Sometimes, I'd be quite happy not having a boyfriend.

Carla comes back, she's got a croissant and another coffee in her hand.

'Hey, mate,' she says, as she sees Klatsche.

'Hey, baby,' says Klatsche.

Oh, OK. Other people have the surname Baby too. Didn't know that.

'Whew,' says Carla, as she sits down next to me, 'I really need to start eating again. I've got a head full of cotton-wool.'

'Want to go and get something proper?' I ask.

'No time,' she says.

'Why, what are you planning?'

'To reopen my café,' she says. 'I need to have the place all systems go by this evening.'

'Carla,' I say, 'isn't that...'

'Leave her,' Klatsche says.

'Right,' she says, 'leave me. You never let me mother you. So don't you try it on me.'

I'd better just keep my trap shut the rest of the day.

DO I KNOW YOU?

I was at a loose end earlier, all alone in my flat, the evening was falling from the sky, there was nobody there, and then I landed up in the Morphine. The Morphine's an electro bunker. A concrete coffin in a cellar beneath the Reeperbahn. It's loud and hard in the Morphine, it's hazy, the air's close, the people are hammered, maybe the air's hammered too because the alcohol is drunk and then sweated straight back out again, and then it just drips off the ceiling. In the Morphine, even your hair gets pissed.

I'm standing in a corner near the bar and I've got a large gin and tonic in my hand.

I need to think.

Carla's not right. Someone has to look after her. Klatsche's doing that. That's OK. That *is* OK. Isn't it? I don't know. It's making me edgy, the whole thing's making me edgy. I get the feeling that Carla and I are slipping away from each other, and the more we do, the more Klatsche and I are slipping weirdly off kilter. Somehow, our friendship triangle is breaking up. At least I can see confusing little cracks in it.

But I'm doing fine. I haven't been raped, or anything else.

And then there are the body parts, about which I couldn't give a flying fuck. I've never experienced that before, not giving a fuck about the dead, not caring who they were or why they had to die.

I feel like whatever I do, I'm in totally the wrong key. As if I'm constantly trying to set foot on the ground, but I can't manage it, either because I get distracted, or because the ground isn't damn well there, where I thought it was. Somehow, I'm bang on the outside, and I don't even know exactly what I'm on the outside of.

I swig from my drink and open my eyes. The lighting system flashes, cutting through the fog and through my eyelids, right into my pupils. And the bass is writhing in my belly.

'Hi? Darling?'

There's a guy in a leather jacket standing there. He's got a cigarette in the corner of his mouth and a stupid grin on his face. I didn't know they let that kind of person in here.

'Do I know you?'

'No, but...'

'Then what's with the darling?' I ask.

'You and me could have a lot of fun together,' he says. 'Darling.'

I kick him on the shin but refrain from punching his lights out, drink up my gin and tonic, go home and wonder if I have any way of getting that place shut down.

The cheek of it.

Calabretta gets back tomorrow.

Thank the good Lord above for that.

It was a Sunday. She was sitting in her bedroom, playing weddings with her Barbie dolls. The Barbies were marrying each other, the blonde one was marrying the dark-haired one, and the ballerina was marrying them too. There was no bridegroom – she didn't have a Ken. Only a Big Jim, a hand-me-down from her cousin. But however hard he tried, Big Jim didn't fit at the altar with those leather things on his legs and his stupid face and his silly karate arm.

She'd made the Barbies' wedding dresses out of paper. They didn't really stay put, they kept falling off all the time, but that didn't matter. In her imagination, they were rustling, swooshing gowns.

The grown-ups were sitting next door in the living room. Her parents had a visitor. A colleague of her father's. She didn't like the man. He smelled of sweat, there was dried spit at the corners of his mouth, and he sometimes sat her on his lap even though she didn't want him to. He just did.

She heard the colleague go to the loo. She heard him pee, she heard the flush, but she didn't hear the taps. Yuck, she thought.

And then he was suddenly standing there in her room.

She was cross with herself for not having shut her door. He bent down to her and stroked her hair. She held her breath.

Hello, he said, sweetie.

She said nothing.

Kept her head down.

Held tight to the blonde Barbie, and the dress fell off again.

Hey, look, he said, boobs. You'll be getting those soon.

PLEASE STOP GETTING IT DIRTY

Hamburg, one p.m., the sun is scorching, and that suits me fine because I've just grilled a couple of girl-traffickers. I was exactly the way I'd have wished to be. I always enjoy reading the charge sheet anyway, but this time it was really fun. At any rate, they're now facing charges of procuration, false imprisonment, human trafficking and establishing a criminal organisation. That's a very good start.

I want to be at the HQ at two, Calabretta's back from Italy and we're meeting for our first official case discussion. So I put my sunglasses on and stroll to the Jungfernstieg. The ferries head north from there, after which it's only a stone's throw to Alsterdorf. I can walk that. If at all possible, I steer clear of public transport. Somehow, I always get lost on buses and trains.

When I was a student in Frankfurt, I once met a dog named Miller. Miller was the exact opposite of me as far as public transport was concerned. Once a day, a butcher gave him a sausage. The only trouble was that Miller lived by the Südbahnhof and the butcher was in Bockenheim.

But that was no problem for Miller – every day, he got the U-Bahn from the Südbahnhof to the Hauptwache where he changed trains for Bockenheim, he'd get out at the Bockenheimer Warte, turn left and left again, and there was his daily sausage. I was seriously impressed yet also deeply mortified because I never, and I mean *never*, get the right train first time.

Over the years, I've stopped confronting public transport.

My boat comes in. Unlike the Elbe ships, the Alster ships are so white and clean and freshly painted that you feel like you've suddenly encountered a swan after years in the company of wild animals. The swan is swimming against a seriously polished backdrop. The trees along the banks of the Alster are gloriously green, the houses and hotels are gloriously posh, and the water from the Alster fountain waves in the air as if it were a lace glove. Sometimes I suspect that this Hamburg was created for TV. For a title sequence with violin music and starched blouses.

As I sit down on one of the delicate benches on deck, a lady in a silver-grey suit looks at me like I'm making her ship dirty.

CODENAME BONE SAW

At twenty past two, I slide in and join the squad at the table. I must have been trapped in a space-time loop on the Alster. Hamburg's second river really can't be trusted.

'*Moin*,' I say.

'*Moin*,' say Brückner and Schulle, Mr Borger the psychologist smiles jovially at me over the top of his glasses, the fabulous Betty Kirschtein from pathology lobs a 'Hey, Riley, how are you?' across the table and Calabretta says '*Servus*.'

Neither of the SOCO guys moves a muscle; they worship their files. They're here without their boss.

'Isn't Mr Hollerieth coming?' I ask, dropping into the free chair beside Calabretta. After a week on the Gulf of Naples, he's as brown as an adder.

'Mr Hollerieth has a bad back,' he says, grinning broadly at me.

I grin back.

Oh yeah.

Calabretta.

Nice to have him back.

'OK,' I say, 'let's get going.'

Brückner points to a folder that's open in front of him.

'We already started, boss.'

Oh, yeah, right.

'Oh, yeah,' I say, 'right.'

'Anyway,' he says, 'we've got two dead men, or rather, the heads, hands and feet of two dead men. There's no trace of the rest. The first was found last Tuesday, the second on Friday. In both cases, they were found in Billwerder Bay. The body parts were packed up in black bin bags, fastened with parcel tape and weighed down with a rounded stone. The weight was just enough for the parcels to sink into the silt. And when the shipping lane was dredged, they reappeared. The name of the witness, the dredger operator, is Heinz Trochowski. He was interviewed after each find and you all have the transcripts in your folders.'

He turns a page.

'The identity of both men has been established. The one found on Tuesday was a certain Dejan Pantelic, who came here from Serbia in the mid-nineties. He was thirty-one years old, a musician with no fixed employment, lived with his girlfriend in Horn. She reported him missing on the Monday of last week. He was last seen the previous Friday in St Pauli, at the Zum Silbersack pub. That was around two a.m., when Pantelic said goodbye to them, apparently heading home. The friends were interviewed and that transcript is in the file too. We also know that the man was considered short-tempered, and even violent, by the people around him. He is said to have punched his girlfriend once or twice, but of course she denies that. Mind you, the guy had never been in any trouble with the law.'

'Is there any connection with the second victim?' I ask.

Brückner shakes his head. 'None. Apart from the fact that he was also last seen in the Kiez and reported missing a few days later,' he says. 'The man was called Jürgen Rost. He was forty-two years old and disappeared three weeks ago. He worked as a driver for a private bus company and lived in a one-bedroom flat in Bahrenfeld. No family, no steady girlfriend, not much history with women. He was last seen by a waitress at the Rutsche, that seedy pub/club place in the Kiez, where he was a regular and generally pretty pissed. In all other respects, he led an entirely unremarkable life.'

'Who reported him missing?' I ask.

'His boss,' he says. 'He got worried when he had to cancel a bus tour because Rost hadn't turned up. Which was very much out of character. According to his boss, he was very conscientious. But he didn't have much else to say about the guy.'

Brückner snaps his folder shut.

'So, that's that from us,' he says.

'Do you have any concrete lines of enquiry?' our psychologist asks. 'Any leads?'

'Close to zero,' says Calabretta, 'we're operating pretty much in the dark.'

He waves his right hand towards the SOCO guys. 'Be my guests.'

The more boring of the two smooths out his file.

'We've got no fingerprints on the packing material and no fibres on the body parts. The perpetrator wore gloves and seems to have cleaned up the victims thoroughly. As if they'd been sandblasted, or at least thoroughly scrubbed. The black bin bags and parcel tape are the standard sort you get in any supermarket. The stones are a bit more interesting. We found traces of grass and compost on them. So they weren't just picked up off the Elbstrand. They're from somewhere cultivated, a park or somebody's garden perhaps.'

The other forensics guy sits up straight.

'And we've got a hair,' he says.

Everyone pricks up their ears.

A hair is always really, really good news.

'A woman's hair, long, dark-blonde, curly.'

'So they didn't clean up quite as thoroughly as all that,'

says Mr Borger. He smiles and makes a note in his psychology book.

'We found the hair on the head of Dejan Pantelic,' says the first forensics guy.

'Maybe he had a little adventure when he set off on his tour of the Kiez,' says Betty Kirschtein.

'Maybe that self-same adventure was his downfall,' says Calabretta, looking at Betty Kirschtein.

He's looking at her a little too long for my taste. Hey ho, it's no secret that Calabretta's trying to get in with our chic pathologist. Everyone's twigged that by now. Betty Kirschtein smiles back briefly, flicks her little red fringe out of her dainty face and then turns her full attention back to studying her fingernails. My feeling is that she isn't remotely interested in Calabretta.

'That's it from us,' says the second forensics guy, and both snap their files shut, as if to order.

Betty Kirschtein looks around. 'Is it my turn?'

'Go ahead,' I say, before poor Calabretta says something stupid and makes a dick of himself.

Our pathologist opens her white folder and I press myself down deeper into my seat. I really like Betty, but I loathe her specialism. I haven't been down to pathology once since Faller hasn't been around. I can't do it without him. I saw my dad lying in pathology after his suicide. He was laid out in the cellar of Frankfurt's university hospital, and I'm not sure which was worse: the night I found him on his desk with a bullet in his head, or the next day, when he lay there on that metal trolley like a wax figure under the neon light.

'The heads and limbs of both victims were detached with considerable skill,' says Betty Kirschtein. 'I'd say that it was done with some kind of bone saw.'

OK, now I feel officially sick.

'Where do you find a thing like that just lying around?' Schulle says. 'A bone saw?'

'Butchers' shops,' says Betty Kirschtein, 'or hospitals.'

I have to concentrate. Don't go and throw up under the conference table. The thought that this might be some kind of doctor with a saw, my God.

'But the amputations weren't the cause of death,' she says. 'The victims were killed via a very precise punch or kick to the bridge of the nose, from below. That drives the nasal bone into the brain, quick and efficient. From there the rest takes care of itself.'

'Who could do a thing like that?' I ask, partly to take my mind off it. 'I mean, you have to learn a kick like that, don't you? I couldn't do it.'

Betty Kirschtein shrugs her shoulders. 'What do the gentlemen here say? Could you do it?'

'Martial arts training,' says Schulle. 'You'd need martial arts training for something like that.'

'Nah,' says the boring forensics man. 'I could do it. Never did karate or anything.'

Everyone, absolutely everyone, looks at him, perplexed.

'You just have to practise at home,' he says, 'on a shop mannequin, for example.'

Nobody says a word.

'What?' he asks. 'Weren't any of you ninja fans?'

Schulle shakes his head.

Calabretta clears his throat and looks at Betty Kirschtein. 'When did the men die? And how long were they in the water?'

This time, he's trying really hard not to stare so much.

'Well,' she says, 'that's hard to say. The parcels were almost airtight, and the skin was a bit wrinkly but there wasn't much decay, I'd guess that they were well chilled, probably right up until they were packed up.' She looks around at us all as she says, 'To be honest, I'm pretty stumped.'

Calabretta turns, a little too quickly in my opinion, to Mr Borger. 'What strikes you about that?'

'We're dealing with a professional,' Mr Borger says, 'that much is certain. Someone who knows what they're doing. Not necessarily in terms of killing, but when handling their tools. This all seems very cool, businesslike and confident.'

'Man or woman?' I ask.

'Can't tell. The brutality, makes me think "man", but the thoroughness and attention to detail say "woman".'

He takes his glasses off and fiddles with them a bit.

'But in any case,' Brückner says, 'we can assume that it's someone who isn't right in the head, can't we?'

'No,' says Mr Borger.

'But why, may I ask, would anyone do anything this warped,' Brückner enquires, 'if he's not insane?'

'Maybe because the situation that he or she finds him- or herself in is an unusual one,' says Mr Borger.

'A situation that requires unusual measures?' asks Betty Kirschtein.

Mr Borger raises his eyebrows and puts his glasses back on. 'Perhaps.'

'OK, come on,' I say, 'cards on the table. Doctor or butcher?'

'Same thing,' says Schulle.

VAFFANCULO

'Grimaldi brown,' says Calabretta, as we drink coffee in his office. He pushes his sunglasses up into his hair, hair which must have copped a fat dollop of styling cream this morning. And it looks a tad longer than usual too. His shirt is dark blue and undone two buttons too far, while on top of his white ribbed vest, a gold cross dangles from a gold chain. Normally, Calabretta keeps his hair short and his shirts buttoned up and never wears sunglasses. A tight leather jacket would be his limit. As if he wanted to clench a fist around the Italian in him. Don't swagger. As if his background was nobody's business but his own. Now it looks as though the sun has utterly burned away the north-German part of his personality. If I didn't know who I was sitting opposite, I'd say 'Mafioso. Nick him.'

'Grimaldi brown, uh-huh,' I say.

'Yo,' he says, rolling to and fro on his chair.

'Nice to have you back,' I say.

'Yo,' he says again, stretching his arms up and his belly

out, and I can see that his shirt's straining slightly. Calabretta sucks the belly in.

'What can you do,' he says, 'two weeks of Zia Giuseppina's pasta twice a day.'

He claps both hands on the little bulge over his belt buckle.

'Brückner and Schulle play football in Altona every Sunday. I'm gonna sign up. They said they could use a good centre-back.'

'Exactly!' yells Schulle from next door. 'A *good* centre-back!'

'Like I said!' Calabretta roars.

I can hear Brückner laughing, and Calabretta says: 'Shut it back there.'

Sometimes I get the feeling these guys work in some kind of men's boarding house.

'The trial began this morning, didn't it, those traffickers?'

'Yeah,' I say, 'the charges are on the table. Tomorrow, the first of the women will make their statements. I hope they don't buckle. I don't think they will. I think it's going to go to plan. You did top work there, Calabretta.'

'Together with you, Riley,' he says. He leans a little closer to me. 'And we still can, even without Faller. There's no need to worry about that.'

'I'm not worried,' I say.

'Yes you are,' says Calabretta.

I stand up, walk over to the open window and light a cigarette. Calabretta's still rolling back and forth on his chair.

'What's our old friend up to these days, anyway? Is he still sitting around under his lighthouse?'

'He's still sitting there,' I say. 'Sitting there fishing.'

I blow smoke out of the window.

'Why's he suddenly taken up fishing?'

'Does him good,' I say.

'*Vaffanculo*,' says Calabretta letting his head fall onto the desk.

I drag on my cigarette. *Vaffanculo*.

'What does that mean?' I ask.

'Go fuck yourself up the arse.'

'What an excellent swear,' I say. Cheap, quick and filling.

'How's Carla?' he asks.

I told Brückner. And Brückner must have told Calabretta.

I throw the butt out of the window.

'That,' I say, 'is *vaffanculo* cubed.'

URBAN GUERILLA

Carla's leaning in the doorway, smoking. She actually has reopened her café. Something about her courage isn't right.

She's wearing straight-cut black trousers and a black T-shirt. Her hair's tied back with a black headscarf, her eyes are made up extra dark. She looks like an urban guerilla. When she sees me coming, she waves and smiles slightly, but her expression remains fierce.

'Hey,' I say.

'Hey,' she says, giving me a hug. She's got thin. Her back is all bony.

'Are you OK?' I ask.

'Not so bad,' she says.

The pavement tables are almost fully occupied. There's nobody sitting inside.

'Can I have a coffee?'

'Sure,' she says.

We go in, she slips behind the bar and fiddles with the coffee machine.

'Say, Carla, you haven't been back in the cellar, have you?'

She shakes her head. 'Nope,' she says, 'I never want to go back down there again. If I could, I'd wall that hole up.'

'Want me to fetch your supplies up for you?' I ask.

'Klatsche's already offered,' she says, 'he was planning to pop round this evening and take care of it.'

'Oh, right,' I say.

'Didn't he say? I thought you'd come together.'

'Nope,' I say, 'he didn't say.'

Would you look at that. My boyfriend and helper of damsels in distress.

'I phoned the lady who took my statement earlier,' Carla says. 'I don't think they've really bothered with it. She just said they'd got a few DNA traces out of my cellar and they'd put them through the computer, the sex-offender records, but unfortunately there weren't any matches. Which is pretty shit.'

She passes me an espresso, sugar and a jug of warm milk.

'We were only at the station on Friday,' I say, 'and today's Monday. They've launched a manhunt and combed your cellar, and now they're investigating. It'll take a while. And probably not much happened over the weekend.'

She immediately blows her top. 'Why not?!'

'Because, like everyone else, they're understaffed and it's

summer, so people are on holiday,' I say. I'm not hearing a word against the police.

'Whose side are you on here?' Her eyes flash.

'Yours,' I say, 'always. You know that.'

'If you were on my side, you'd call them right now and put the pressure on.'

'I can't put any pressure on,' I say. 'I don't call the shots there. It's not my department.'

'Department?' she asks. 'Since when have you given a stuff about that?'

'I'm not messing with other people's work,' I say.

Carla turns away and thumps the coffee machine. There's a wave of rage towering over the back of her neck.

'Carla,' I say.

'Fine,' she says quietly, 'it's OK.'

She turns around and looks at me, and I can see that absolutely nothing is OK.

MUSIC IN THE BACKGROUND

As I set off for home, the sun is a red ball hanging over St Pauli, it's just on the point of dropping behind the roof-tops. I went back to the office and got myself ready for tomorrow. I've been over the witness statements again and again, line by line. If the girls repeat what they said when they were interviewed in anything like the same terms, the outlook's seriously poor for the Brothers Pimp.

It's a warm evening and life is whooping in the streets. St Pauli resembles a massive mob of friends, there's chatter, laughter, music everywhere. I feel like a beer, and I ring Klatsche's doorbell. He's not there. I pull out my phone and call him. It takes a while for him to answer.

'Hey, Riley,' he says.

'Come for a beer with me?' I ask.

'The question is,' he says, 'will you come for a beer with me?'

In the background I can hear voices and music. It sounds like he's at one of those bloody beach clubs.

'Where are you?' I ask.

'At the beach,' he says. 'Carla's here too. Coming?'

'I have to be up early tomorrow,' I say, and, 'give her my love.'

She went swimming three times a week. She was fast, she had stamina, she could dive. It was so much fun. And then there was this boy. He had red hair and freckles. When he was at the pool, it was even more fun.

Having a shower was more fun than it used to be too. It was nice to wash her hair, to comb it and blow it dry. To rub cream into her skin and then slip into clean underwear. Sometimes, when she was alone in the changing room, she even put mascara on.

One day, when she was under the shower, letting the warm water run over her a bit longer than necessary, she suddenly felt somebody there. Somebody watching her, watching her very closely. She opened her eyes. Standing in the doorway to the girls' shower was the lifeguard. He was standing there, looking at her like she belonged to him.

She wanted to tell him to go away, but she couldn't utter a word. She hastily grabbed her towel and held it over her body.

Hey, you, said the lifeguard, don't always have such long showers.

TEN PUNTERS A DAY

She turned eighteen two weeks ago. When we pulled her out of the backroom brothel on the Grosse Freiheit, she was a bundle of fear, clinging clothes, colourful boots, cheap make-up and badly healed cuts. Now the make-up's gone, she's wearing jeans and trainers and a blue T-shirt with white polka dots. She's a young girl again. And that way, her story makes an even more brutal impact.

She was sixteen when the guys lured her away from her home, told her about horses, about the golden west, about how much money she could earn there. Even as a waitress or a dancer, she'd be rich in two years. And then, they said, she'd have no problem providing for her family in Romania. And, they couldn't promise anything, obviously, but with her looks, she might make it as a model.

Today, she says she was stupid. She's way too short to be a model.

I don't think she was stupid. She was just young and she had no dad at home, only an overwhelmed mum, three little brothers and a grandma who was half dead.

Things in Hamburg began with beatings and continuous rape. She was broken in over two weeks. After that, she says, she didn't want to go on living, so she just did whatever, it didn't matter either way. She'd lost all sense of her body and her soul and of justice. She managed an average of ten punters a day but didn't see a cent. She slept and lived in the same hole that the punters came to – in her two years of captivity, she only went outside four times, under supervision. She didn't know that she could have screamed for help. The men had told her that in Germany, women who worked as prostitutes were put in camps.

As she tells her story, her voice sounds like she's not talking about herself. As if it had all happened to somebody else.

SMOOTH OPERATOR

I feel a little stab somewhere around the heart as I see Klatsche.

'Hey, baby,' he says, taking my hand.

'Don't call me baby,' I say, pulling my hand away.

He raises his eyebrows and says: 'What's wrong now? Are we back to square one?'

Carla comes out of the kitchen and gives me a kiss on the cheek.

'Hey,' she says. 'Why didn't you come and join us on the beach yesterday?'

If only I'd steered clear of here. It is actually possible to spend your bloody lunch break in other places. Carla looks at me a beat longer than usual. I think she's spotted what's going on here.

'We'll talk later, OK?' she says, laying her hand on my cheek.

'OK,' I say.

'Want something to eat?' she asks.

It's busy, the café is rammed. I'm hungry. But I don't want to be a nuisance.

'Can I go into the kitchen and make myself something?' I ask.

'Sure,' she says and smiles at me, warm and soft and the way Carla smiles, the way she always used to smile before this shit happened.

I make my way to the kitchen. Klatsche lifts his hands and shakes his head. Then he slips down from his barstool and comes after me.

'What's wrong?' he asks.

I don't answer, just open the fridge. In the door, there's an open bottle of white wine. I pull it out, take a glass, pour a good glassful and take a gulp. Klatsche grabs my forearm.

'What's wrong with you, Chastity Riley?'

I'd like to say that I don't know what's wrong, exactly, but that it hurts to see him, and that it hurts just as much not to see him, and that I think we've come to the end of our fling. I say, 'Nothing's wrong'.

'You're pissed off,' he says.

'I'm just not in the mood for coupledom right now,' I say, and I could kick myself for saying *that* of all things.

'And I'm not in the mood for playing silly buggers,' he says. 'That's not us. We've always been honest with each other, if you recall.'

I look at him and I have to really watch myself to stop

the tears welling up. I just don't get what's going on here. I'm out of my depth with this lovey-dovey shit.

Klatsche shakes his head again and says: 'Oh, screw you, Chastity.'

Then he walks back out into the café. I take my wine glass and follow him because I don't know what else to do.

Just before he gets to the bar, Klatsche suddenly stops. I almost run him down.

Rocco Malutki is here. He's sitting at the bar, he's making sheep's eyes at Carla but she's not responding.

'Malutki, you madman!'

Klatsche sets a course towards his friend. He and Rocco met in jail. Klatsche was doing time for burglary, Rocco for a thousand and one petty frauds. Rocco Malutki – the classic smooth operator. The kind of guy who's good-looking, even if you can't quite put your finger on why, who spends most of his time in the company of beautiful women – but you couldn't say anything for certain there either. Who these women even are, for instance, what kind of relationship he has with them, and what's even going on there. Plus he's got brains. It was his idea for Klatsche to set up as a locksmith, seeing how good he is at opening doors. Klatsche says that without Rocco, he'd still be doing one break-in after another, and getting sent down every year or two. Rocco slides down from his stool and spreads his arms wide. He's wearing an old pair of pinstriped trousers, which slip down a little from his bony hips, and one of those Sicilian flat caps, the kind Robert de Niro wears as a young Vito Corleone. His light-brown curls crinkle out from under the cap, his beard is a little too wispy to count as proper designer stubble, and when he laughs you can see the slight gap between his long front teeth, which makes him look extra cunning. He's a wide boy, heart and soul, and can make music like an angel. He plays the piano, sax and guitar. He doesn't own any of these instruments. Officially, because he's opposed to it. To owning stuff. The truth is that he couldn't even afford a recorder. Rocco Malutki is as poor as a church mouse.

His mother was a celebrity, a Kiez great, the most beautiful of all the whores, and unlike most, she really never had a pimp. Her ancestors were part Spanish and part Argentinian, but she wasn't too sure which were which. She was dark and wild and wouldn't be told what to do. When she got pregnant in her mid-thirties, she gave up her job and opened a little café on the Reeperbahn. She ran the joint until she died a few years ago. The café used to be a fixture in the Kiez, and the plan was for Rocco to take it over. But unfortunately, he was doing another couple of months inside when his mother died and she hadn't provided for that situation. She never had admitted to herself that her son had a tendency to get into trouble.

Rocco's father was a Polish musician. He played the violin, here one day, there the next. He disappeared without warning when Rocco was a few months old. Rocco's mother never got involved with another man after that, but she wouldn't say a bad word about the Polish violinist either. To this day, she's revered like a saint in St Pauli.

Not even Rocco knows exactly how he makes a living. He lives a bit off his mother's fame, a bit off his music, the occasional spot of wheeling and dealing – and the fact that the sly dog's so sharp and so fucking good-looking can't him do any harm either.

I've always kind of liked him.

'So,' says Klatsche, 'how was Berlin, man?'

'Boring,' says Rocco, pushing his cap back a touch.

He looks kind of knackered around the eyes. Like everyone who's spent a while in Berlin.

I'd like to give Rocco a hug too but I have no desire to keep trotting after Klatsche like an idiot, so I stay hanging around in the doorframe like an even bigger idiot.

'Chastity, hotshot legal eagle, come here, let me kiss you!'

'Hey, Rocco,' I say, pulling myself together and walking over. 'How are you?'

'Lousy,' he says, putting on a heart-rending face, 'I'm suffering. There I was, away for a whole year, in the big, cold city, not looking at a single woman because all I could think of was your beautiful friend Carla, and then I come back and grovel before her in the Hamburg dust, and she's as cold-hearted and unkind as ever.'

Carla's standing behind the bar with a dangerous slant to her eyebrows, sorting coffee cups into the dishwasher. I light a cigarette and try to smile. Rocco Malutki, what do you want from me? Am I in charge of other people's emotions now too? I don't even know where to pigeonhole my own.

'I have to make a phone call,' I say, walking outside and ringing Calabretta.

'Chastity,' he says, 'nice of you to call.'

'How's it going?' I ask.

'We're poking around in the fucking dark here,' he says.

I wipe the sweat off my brow. It really is about time it rained again.

She and a few friends were hanging around by the dodgems, watching. Like everyone did. There were two boys who drove extra wildly. Caused all these massive crashes etc. One of them smiled every time he swerved past her. Eventually, she smiled back – she thought he was cute. He got out and bought her candyfloss. He strolled around the fairground with her. He paid for her ride on the Ferris wheel. He was nineteen. When the big wheel stopped for a while, right up at the top, he started to kiss her. Touched her under her jumper. She didn't really mind but things were going a bit fast for her. Then, suddenly, his hand was in her trousers. She didn't want that, pushed his hand away. He wouldn't be pushed away. The hand stayed where it was. He said: Don't make such a fuss. I just want a quick fuck.

TRENCH-COAT WEATHER

A bank of cloud has rolled in overnight. The Elbe looks cold and dirty. Dark, bad-tempered, churned up.

'He was only young,' says Calabretta.

'Mid-twenties, tops,' says Brückner.

The three of us are standing around the body, waiting, yet again, for the SOCO squad. Our colleagues whose beat this is have taped the little shipyard off.

The shipyard worker who found the body has broken down. He's being looked after at home by one of our psychologists. Finally, a normal witness.

The dead man's face looks kind of elegant, almost arrogant, even. It fits with the fine, well-looked-after hands. His light-blond hair is a bit longer at the front than the back – it must have been a style that required slicking back off his face. He's wearing a pale-blue Ralph Lauren shirt and the kind of jeans that can't be had for less than two hundred and fifty big ones. The boy looks like he had no money worries.

And he's come to us in one piece.

I look up to the heavens. The clouds are sinking ever lower. The wind's blowing steadily. Hamburg summer is back. I should have brought my trench coat.

OBJECTS OF SPECULATION

'So,' says Mr Hollerieth, flipping open his file and smoothing down the papers within. He's occupied the place at the head of the table and, judging by the look on his face, he's planning to throw his weight around. His back must be OK again then. At any rate, he's sitting quite at his ease in his chair, and his lips always have that uptight twist to them.

I'm sitting between Calabretta and Brückner, Schulle's not here, he's got the photos of our latest floater and is searching through the CID files for him. Our man can't have been deposited among the missing persons yet, his condition was too good for that, he just looked too fresh.

Mr Borger is sucking on an ice lolly. Betty Kirschtein is flicking through a newspaper.

'So,' says Hollerieth again.

'Yes,' says Calabretta, 'how's it looking? Have we got anything?'

'Not really,' says Hollerieth. 'No papers, no credit cards. Just a bit of cash.'

'We knew that much already,' mutters Brückner.

Hollerieth is instantly offended, snaps his file shut, turns down his mouth and stares out of the window. Calabretta glances imploringly at Brückner.

'Sorry,' says Brückner.

Hollerieth keeps frowning as he devotes his attention to the window for a moment longer, then he turns back to us.

'He wasn't in there long,' he says.

'Crabs hadn't started to bite?' Calabretta asks.

'No crabs on the body,' says Hollerieth. 'And the man is pretty much unscathed in other respects too. I could imagine him still being alive yesterday evening. What do you say, Ms Kirschtein?'

'Bingo,' says Betty Kirschtein. 'Time of death was somewhere between midnight and two. The body was in the water for no more than four, five hours.'

'How did he die?' I ask.

'The same as the two lads we've only got bits of,' she says. 'Well aimed punch or kick to the bridge of the nose, bone in the brain, over and out.'

'So presumably the same perpetrator?' asks Calabretta.

'Well, working that bit out would be your job,' she says.

Calabretta flinches ever so slightly. Nobody else sees. But he does.

Jeez, Betty.

'Mr Borger?' I ask.

He's finished his lolly and he's chewing on the stick.

'If it is one and the same killer,' Mr Borger says, 'he's getting either careless or nervous.'

'Which do you think?'

'Nervous,' he says. 'We didn't put a media blackout in place. The papers have been up to their eyeballs in the first two finds for days. And given how thoroughly and cleanly packed the parcels were, I don't think the killer would get sloppy for no reason. To me, it looks as though someone was pretty surprised that the body parts were found. They were intended to sink without trace. And seeing that that didn't work, they've suddenly got frantic and just thrown the body into the water without any further shenanigans, right behind the first jetty in the freeport area. Seems like it's no longer worth all the hassle of chopping them up and packing them up and making them disappear...'

He puts the lolly stick down and takes off his glasses.

'Do you have any idea,' I say, 'why our perpetrator kills? It's a pretty serious body count now.'

'I haven't a clue,' he says. 'But I think the killing and the dismembering are unconnected. The way all the men die doesn't fit with what is done to the first two corpses. It seems to me that those two were killed on the spur of the moment, physical, quick, as if it happened in a short, fierce fight. But then the remains are so clean – professional, routine work that can only have been done using a machine. I'm going out on a bit of a limb here, but I'm saying that we're dealing with two perpetrators. They're very different, but something links them.'

I can't help thinking back to the uniformed police-woman who said something very much along those lines. Smart girl.

'Misandry?' asks Hollerieth, making a face like he's just been given a hot enema.

Betty Kirschtein rolls her eyes.

'I wouldn't go that far,' says Mr Borger, 'or we'd be facing severely abused, tortured bodies down there on the slab. Hatred always goes hand in hand with torture. Our victims were dispatched quickly and painlessly. But all the same, this is evidently about – and yes, targeting – men.'

'So was only one of them involved with this morning's corpse then?' Calabretta asks. 'Because the dismember-ment specialist was unavailable? Or how should we be visualising this?'

Mr Borger puts his glasses back on and says: 'Speculation.'

'People,' Calabretta says, rubbing his face with both hands, 'we have absolutely nothing to go on here. And we've got three dead men inside a week. This is moving towards squeaky-bum time.'

'OK,' I say, 'in which case, I suggest rolling out the big guns, whatever the cost. Put a squad together, Calabretta, and go through every hospital and butcher's shop in the city with a fine-tooth comb, along with any other place that any such thing as a bone saw might be lying around. If your guys come across anything weird, call me and I'll get a search warrant for them right away. On top of which, turn the rubbish dumps upside down and send the divers back out into all the relevant sections of the port. We need the bodies of Pantelic and Rost.'

'Good,' says Calabretta. 'That'll put a bit of a rocket up things.'

The door opens, Schulle comes in. He's got a few photos from the police records department in his hand.

'Got him,' he says.

Well, now I can't wait to see what our dead man has been up to.

NOT ON GOOD TERMS

I always forget that we're still in Hamburg here. And I can't believe that these places exist, that people live like this, that they take it seriously. I know that a few of my colleagues from the prosecution service actually do live like this, in this neck of the woods even, but never in my wildest dreams would I want to live in such a place. It's twisted.

Calabretta does a few laps around Innocentia Park, then swears as he has to double-park. The boy from Altona can hardly hide his disgust either.

'These fucking fat-cat houses,' he says, 'they stick in my craw. Money to burn, but no parking spaces for the police.'

He's seriously pissed off.

'Keep your hair on,' I say, 'don't lose your cool over a bit of bling.'

If the lady and gentleman of the house are about to learn that their son will never again sit down to meals with them at the mahogany dining table, they need to be faced with a level-headed police inspector and not a raging madman. Because then they'll be poor, no matter how much money they've got.

We walk past a sharply coiffed hedge and stop outside a six-foot wrought-iron gate. Over our heads to our left is a camera. In front of our noses is a golden bellpush and a golden nameplate. The nameplate reads *von Lell*. I press the bell, Calabretta whips out his ID.

'Hello?'

The intercom sounds very clipped.

'Hamburg CID,' says Calabretta, holding his ID up to the camera. 'May we come in?'

There's a buzz and a click, and the gate swings open.

Ahead of us, a path of anthracite-grey gravel snakes away to a pale-grey, three-storey mansion. The façade is clad with just the right amount of elegant white stucco. To our left and right extend perfect lawns, with rose bushes humourlessly pruned and standing to attention. Standing in the front doorway is a man in grey trousers, a white shirt and a navy tank top. The man looks as though he's spent his life doing business with the Russians. His expression is heartless.

Calabretta introduces us. Mr von Lell doesn't bat an eyelash. I ask if we can come in. Mr von Lell eyes us, nods, steps aside. Calabretta enquires whether Mrs von Lell is at home. No, she's out at bridge. I almost knock over a vase. Sorry.

Mr von Lell sits down in an armchair just inside the front door; whether we like it or not, we stand – there are no armchairs for us.

'I'm afraid we have come to bring you some bad news,' says Calabretta.

I think Mr von Lell's right eyebrow might have moved upward a fraction.

'It's about your son Hendrik,' I say.

Now the eyebrow does twitch.

'Hendrik is dead. He was murdered.'

He shuts his eyes and folds his hands in his lap. Then he opens his eyes again and looks first at me and then at Calabretta.

'How?' he asks.

'Probably a blow to the head,' says Calabretta. 'He was killed instantly. He didn't suffer.'

Mr von Lell nods. He never stops looking at us and his expression hasn't changed in the last five minutes, since he opened the door to us. He reacts so sparingly to the news that I'm not sure he's grasped what we're talking about.

'We will let you know as soon as your son's body is re-leased,' says Calabretta.

'If you could kindly deal with everything via our lawyer,' says Mr von Lell, handing Calabretta a business card. The boot.

'I'm afraid we have to ask you a few more questions,' says Calabretta.

Mr von Lell nods and crosses his legs.

Calabretta asks the usual questions about friends and enemies, whether Hendrik had changed recently, and who he might have been out with yesterday evening. All Mr von Lell has to say to any of that is: 'My son and I were not on good terms.'

'But he lived here?' I ask.

Mr von Lell nods. Good grief. What must that have been like, living under the same roof. I'm happier with no father than with one like this.

'Six months ago, a young woman accused your son of sexual assault,' I say.

'The investigation was closed,' he says, and suddenly he looks like a lizard, dry and thin-lipped.

'I know,' I say, 'but I'd like to hear your opinion on the matter.'

'Utter nonsense,' he says. A vein appears on his temple. The vein is throbbing and that is, by some margin, the strongest reaction I've seen from him to this point.

'I must ask you,' he says, 'also to discuss this with our lawyer. May I show you out?'

Indisputably the boot.

'There's no need,' I say, 'we can find our own way to the door.'

Once we're outside again, I feel my shoulders relaxing, the icy rigidity in the back of my neck slowly melting.

'That was close,' says Calabretta.

'Seriously close,' I say.

We came within a whisker of freezing to death.

I light a cigarette.

'Have we got time for a quick coffee?'

My watch says: No. There's a press conference back at the police HQ in fifteen minutes.

My inner leopardess says: 'We can squeeze it in.'

UP HERE IN THE NORTH

Our press officer is sitting in the centre with Calabretta sitting to his left and me sitting to his right, sitting on the chairs in front of him are the ladies and gentlemen of the press. We're almost through with this thing. I get the feeling that every question has been asked.

'Will that be all?' asks our press officer, looking around the room.

My skull is buzzing. I urgently need some fresh air and a smoke.

There's a guy in the third row, fourth chair from the left, in a weird eighties' get-up. He's wearing a pale jacket with shoulder pads, jeans that are too high at the waist and some kind of lumberjack shirt. He puts his hand up. Oh no.

'Gunnar Steiss, *Bergedorfer Tageblatt*,' he says.

'Go ahead,' says our press officer.

The guy pushes his glasses up a bit with his middle finger, the way people push their glasses up when they're not doing it to see better but to draw attention to the fact that they're wearing glasses. Then with his left hand, he strokes his hair out of his face, and that too is a confusing relic of the worst decade for fashion in the last century. Blond and straggly, with a kind of bum-crack parting down the middle. All in all, he reminds me a bit of Robin Gibb. In his right hand, he's holding a pen, which he raises slightly at the same moment that he strokes back his hair, he's making a massive wave before he finally starts to ask his question.

'Ms Riley, what interests me, up here in the north, is how it is that you, seeing as you're half American after all, don't you think that it's both depressing and damning that this keeps happening, that first and foremost, the crudely putrid dregs of society keep revealing themselves up here in the north, shouldn't you therefore, representing the power of the state, should you not intervene and point the moral finger in warning, to remind our people more force-fully of their civic responsibilities? I mean, what on earth have things come to, up here in the north?'

He pushes his glasses up again, but not with his hand this time, but by wrinkling his nose, and in the process, he bares an incredible picket fence of front teeth.

Oh, for the love of Mike. A provincial columnist.

PORT NOISES

The bank of clouds from this morning is a little more see-through now. In a few places, the grey sky has even turned some pretty shades of pink and almost blue. There's practically no wind. As if the weather has been tired out by the day so far.

Faller is sitting by his lighthouse, looking at the water. The atmosphere resembles a painting by Caspar David Friedrich. Pensive, one hundred per cent German romanticism. The little spit of concrete land, sticking out into the harbour basin, still bang in the centre of the city, within spitting distance of the Michel and the other church towers. The ships on the mirror-calm water at the landing bridges diagonally opposite us. The clifflike Kaispeicher in red brick. The freeport in the background with its shipyards and docks, black with a touch of rust here and there. And up ahead, on the tip of the spit, the red-and-white-ringed lighthouse, not even as tall as a person standing on somebody else's shoulders. At its feet: the old man and the Elbe.

A tall ship will come sailing around the corner any minute.

Faller's not fishing today. He's listening to music. He's got a portable CD player lying beside him and large silver headphones on his ears. His straw hat is lying next to the CD player. From close up, he no longer cuts a romantic figure. He looks like a badly aged DJ.

'Hey,' I say.

He doesn't respond. I tap him on the shoulder. He takes the headphones off and glances up at me, then looks back at the water.

'Chastity,' he says, and his voice is as clear and calm as if he'd swallowed a Buddha.

'How are you?' I ask.

'Fine,' he says, 'I'm fine.'

'Aren't you fishing anymore?' I ask.

'Am I still fishing?' he asks in return.

'No,' I say.

'Well then,' he says.

I sit next to him on the quay wall. The port noises are incredibly clear today too. To the far left there's a puckering, nearer left there's a hammering, straight ahead there's a horn. Nothing mingles.

'What are you listening to?' I ask.

He takes the headphones from his lap and puts them on me. Sounds like submarine noises.

'Submarine noises?' I ask.

'Whale song,' he says. 'I've got birdsong too. Want to hear that one?'

'No,' I say, 'thank you.'

I hand him back the headphones. Uh-huh. Whale song. If it soothes your soul – go for it. I've resolved not to interfere. Faller will know what does him good. He smiles at me.

'We've got another dead man,' I say.

'A whole body?' he asks. 'In one piece?'

I nod. 'But Mr Borger thinks it's the same perpetrator,' I say, 'or possibly the same two perpetrators. He thinks they're working as a pair.'

'Hm,' says Faller. 'The ladies are going at quite a rate.'

'Ladies?' I ask. 'What makes you think we're dealing with women?'

'Smells that way,' he says. He taps the tip of his nose. 'I'm almost certain of it.'

'Why?' I ask. 'Because it's men who are dying?'

'No idea,' he says, 'perhaps. But I'd bet my tatty old heart on it.'

He looks at me. There's a glint in his eyes.

'Faller,' I say, 'are you planning a comeback?'

He looks back at the water, lights himself a Roth-Händle and says: 'Keep an eye on the gulls, Chastity, always keep a sharp eye on the gulls.'

There are five of them on the move in the sky above us. They're gliding through the still air and they look very comfortable. Until one of them picks up speed. First it pulls upward, then it plunges down, and *pow*, it pulls a fish out of the water.

THERE'S STILL A LIGHT ON AT KLATSCHE'S

It's dark when I turn on to my street. The chains of lights outside the cafés and the upcycling shop and the super-hard-core bike shop are all off. The Kandie Shop's hosting a party down at the port tonight, everyone's there so they all shut early. There's no one standing on the pavement using a burning dustbin as a barbecue like normal either. And the corner where my street begins has got boring since the Bar Centrale closed down. A cocktail bar opened in its place recently, but not a soul drinks cocktails there. Could have told them that. Cocktails are way OTT.

An old woman comes towards me. She's wearing grey trousers and a pale-grey blazer with an even paler-grey blouse beneath it. Her clothes are immaculately ironed but there's a stain or two on them. The stains are either very old and won't come out, or the woman just can't see them these days. She's hunched, pushing one of those rolling frame things. Hanging from the right handlebar is a black bag and written in gold letters on the bag is *Vanity Fair*. She stops and looks up into the evening sky and says: 'How lovely. It's snowing. It snows so rarely in St Pauli.'

I tell her that I'm pleased to see the snow too and try to keep my smile as free of sympathy as possible. When I see old women walking around the city looking so lost, I start feeling lonely. I phone Carla.

'Hello?'

'It's me,' I say. 'What are you doing?'

'I'm out for a stroll,' she says.

'Where, who with and why?' I ask.

Carla never goes for strolls.

'With Rocco,' she says 'to the Deichtorhallen. We're looking for the palm trees? You know, those three starved things that used to be there at the crossroads, they're gone and we wanted to check on them.'

'OK,' I say, 'OK.'

I hang up. Somehow, I'm not in the mood for corn right now. And that sounds bloody corny to me.

I get a beer from the crappy snack bar. The place is always full, everyone makes a beeline for it, goes crazy for it. I don't get the appeal. I'd never eat there. Everything tastes like an old dishrag. Smells like one too. But you can buy beer. In bottles.

As I come out with two beers in my hand, I see that there's still a light on at Klatsche's. For a moment, I'm glad that he's in, we could have a drink together, I think, and not talk about it. Then I see him walking across his living room and I also see the girl who's throwing back her head and laughing. She looks sweet, young and cheerful, and I can guess how clear and bell-like she sounds.

I get myself into my flat on the double, put Johnny Cash on the record player and turn all the dials up to ten.

She was on her way to visit her boyfriend, who was at uni in another city. She was taking the train like she did every other weekend. There weren't many people on the train. It was winter and it had been dark for an hour. She was sitting alone in the compartment, reading a newspaper. She was sitting by the window because she found it cosier, even though you could hardly see a thing. She didn't pay much attention when the door opened and somebody sat down with her in her compartment, she was so engrossed in her paper.

But the guy chatted her up anyway.

She was polite, looked up for a moment and smiled.

The guy was about fifty, wearing a dark-blue hat and a shabby, dark-blue coat with a greasy collar with a lot of dandruff on it. His glasses looked like they hadn't been cleaned for weeks. He'd sat on the middle seat, diagonally opposite her, and he'd stretched his legs right across the compartment. If she'd wanted to get out, she'd have had to climb over him. He'd shut the compartment door and evidently closed the curtains too, she now realised.

She tried to ignore him and to keep reading.

But he had his eyes on her the whole time, kept chatting to her. She just didn't respond.

At some point, he started breathing heavily while he stared at her, hand in his trousers.

When he was finished, he asked her if she'd go for a drink with him in the buffet car.

THE GOING OUT FOR DINNER TYPE

I once swore that I would never, absolutely never, drink the filter coffee in the court canteen ever again. But when the day feels this bitter anyway, it makes no difference. You might as well get that stewed stuff inside you during a break in proceedings.

'Cup or mug?'

'Mug,' I say.

'There's milk and sugar at the till.'

'Thanks.'

It tastes revolting. I sit at a table and call Calabretta. He doesn't answer. I snap my phone shut and put it down on the table in front of me.

'I'd always answer if you rang me.'

Ah. The nice barrister. I'm not just saying that, I mean it. He's a good sort. Takes on totally hopeless cases for people with no money. And he gets a lot of them off, because he's not just a nice barrister, he's a good one too. And he doesn't even care that his clients can never pay him. They don't make them like that anymore.

'Since when can you afford a phone?' I ask.

'I beg your pardon, Madam Prosecutor,' he says, 'here is exhibit A.'

He pulls a battered old Nokia from his trouser pocket. They haven't made them like *that* for a long time either.

'May I join you?'

'Of course,' I say.

He puts a tray on the table and takes a seat. On the tray there's a pot of full-fat yoghurt, beside which is a spoon. That's it. I've noticed before how little he eats. I honestly think it's all he can afford.

'I'm still saving up for dinner with you,' he says.

He's been trying to go out for dinner with me for years. And I've been bottling out for years. I'm just not the going out for dinner type.

He rips the tinfoil off his yoghurt pot with a flourish, digs in his spoon and eats as if it were a luscious roast wild boar. There's something Peter Pan-like about it. And seeing him sitting there, with his bony shoulders in his white shirt, his dark, ultrashort hair and his cheerful, intelligent eyes, I think: maybe I am the going out for dinner type after all. Maybe then I'll forget the image from last night, of Klatsche and the girl. I know that he gets his hands on someone else now and then, but somehow this time it's even more annoying than normal. Besides, I'd never seen it live before.

'Have you scraped the cash together then?' I ask.

'I can always scrounge some off a friend.'

'OK,' I say.

'OK, we'll go out for dinner?'

I nod.

'You can tell your friend to cough up the dosh.'

'That's great, I'll pick you up this evening at eight.'

Doing the thing properly. Not bad.

'Great,' I say, 'see you at eight.'

Then I stand up and try Calabretta again. He's still not answering.

DISCO RESTAURANT

This afternoon, I was looking forward to having dinner with the barrister and, earlier on when he picked me up from home, I was still in a good mood. Why shouldn't I have a nice evening with a nice guy now and then? Now I remember why – something always goes seriously wrong.

I can't believe what a weird joint the barrister has dragged me to. I know the place, but, like everyone else in St Pauli, only from the outside. Nobody would willingly set foot in here. It's a foreign body, an aggressor. Its mere presence fucks the area up. The Kiez residents hated the thing even before people were seriously talking about turning the old factory into a restaurant. The mere idea of putting something money-related on that site – I'm ashamed to be here. I hope nobody sees me.

We're sitting in an alcove at a white, square table, the table is kind of like a white wave in plexiglass, and hanging over us is a gigantic, cream-coloured device that's half fabric lamp and half plastic womb. Gives no light, but is supposed to exude atmosphere. I can't see a thing, I'm sitting as stiff as broccoli in my seat, staring from the barrister to the gloomy red brick walls and back again, and not knowing what to say.

'Hello, I'm Jason and I'll be looking after you this evening.'

Jason's black shirt is so tight that it's straining at the buttons on his chest. And it's glossy. Like his hair, his fingernails and his face. Jason needs to piss off and never come back.

'Thank you, Jason,' says the barrister, taking possession of the menus, putting them aside and looking at me.

'I'm sorry,' he says.

'That's OK,' I say.

'I thought this place was the shit,' he says.

'I'm afraid it's just shit,' I say.

'It's hideous,' he says. 'It's a disco restaurant.'

I open the menu. The first dish in the fish section is called Pierced Perch.

'Pierced perch,' I say. 'What must it feel like to have to cook a thing like that?'

'We can leave now, go somewhere else, honestly.'

He looks agonised.

I lean over to him so as not to have to yell so much the whole time. The music isn't just insanely bad, it's also insanely loud. And that in itself is always a strong argument never to eat at a place again. Food and loud music don't mix. Any more than a hairdresser's and loud music, a newspaper kiosk and loud music, or a dentist and loud music. They just don't go.

'Let's go through with this,' I say, 'but on two conditions.'

I don't want him to feel bad. He doesn't deserve that.

'One, we start drinking right away,' I say, 'and two, I'm paying.'

The barrister nods. He knows that it's not open to discussion. And that I have more money than him.

'OK,' I say, 'let's order some beer and something to eat. What will you have?'

'Gentleman's Delight,' he says, 'which is salsiccia with fried potatoes.'

At twenty-two euros fifty, that's the cheapest dish on the menu.

The barrister sees what I'm thinking.

'Hey,' he says, 'I like sausages.'

This Jason bloke comes back to our table and wants to know how he can indulge us. The barrister orders two beers and his sausage. I go for fish, stuffed with herbs. Not pierced.

As Jason disappears behind the bar, where he's more concerned with checking his hairstyle than getting on with liberating our beer from the tap, the barrister and I turn our attention to the other diners.

'Dickheads,' I say, 'they're all dickheads.'

'And Barbie dolls,' says the barrister.

It really isn't nice. The men are all wearing that slightly sweaty business look with tight shirt collars and shiny suits. Hair either shaved or slicked back to the skull. Dickheads. The women's big hair makes them a menace across the board. Prosecco-over-ice robots.

Our beer arrives, not brought by Jason, but by a woman with blondish curls. And curves that could officially be classed as a weapon. She doesn't introduce herself to us, she says nothing at all, she just hands us two beers. Yet as she does, she exudes – entirely incidentally – so much sex appeal that my mouth dries out, while the barrister is more concerned with not slobbering down his shirt. And he's not the only one. Every man in the room is devouring the waitress with their eyes, totally losing their composure, I've never seen anything like it. The woman is undoubtedly beautiful, but there's more to it than that. It seems like there's something else driving these men so crazy, something ancient, archaic, like the phone's ringing in the reptilian part of their brains. Some of them are on the verge of ripping off their shirts and falling upon her. Only their ties are holding them back.

The waitress herself seems uneasy about it all. But then again. In one instant, she seems helpless in the face of what she stirs up in the men, while in the next she's aggressive and arrogant, and then she moves as slowly through the room as if a James Bond title sequence had been built into her body.

'Show's over,' I say to the barrister.

The poor man is totally out of it.

He hasn't even noticed that Mr Jason has arrived with our food.

'Oh,' the barrister says, 'I'm sorry.'

'Never mind,' I say.

He can't help it.

Jason puts the plates down and I think he's acting kind of insulted.

'Thank you,' I say.

He tilts his head on one side, turns and trots away.

My fish looks good. Plump, crisp skin, on a mountain of greenery. They needn't have bothered with the flowers in its mouth though.

The barrister stares at his salsiccia.

'What?' I ask.

'Insane,' he says.

The sausage is a deep brown, with almost a hint of red. It looks like gingerbread. The potatoes shimmer golden yellow, studded with glossy rosemary. To me, it looks one notch too heavy, but I can imagine that, if you're always hungry and you like that kind of thing, it looks amazing.

'I love this kind of thing,' says the barrister.

'Dig in, then,' I say.

We clink glasses, each of us takes a big swig of beer and we start eating. The barrister cuts into his meat, it smells of thyme and nutmeg, of chilli and pepper. It really does smell very good. He sticks a piece in his mouth, chews, his eyes widen.

'And?' I say.

'I don't know,' he says.

'Isn't it good?' I ask.

'No, no,' he says, 'sensational. But unlike anything I've ever eaten.'

He chews. The speakers above our heads are now blaring bargain-basement techno.

'Hmm,' he says.

He pops another piece into his mouth and smiles in delight.

'Amazing. Almost like ... wild boar...? How's your fish?'

I apply my fork, peel back the crisp skin. The flesh is white and delicate, but firm. The herbs smell of a huge garden in the south of France. I have a try. It tastes fresh and green and very cautiously of lime with this delicate hint of coconut.

I shake my head.

'I honestly can't believe how good this food is.'

We clink. After all, we had resolved to drink.

I look around again. There really are only idiots in here. I don't get it. This amazing food just doesn't belong here.

ONE LAST CIGARETTE

It's getting light, there's the first grey-blue stripe to be seen on the horizon and the stars are slowly clearing the field. I'm sitting at my open window, smoking. I can't sleep, had too many vodka and tonics after dinner at the bar in the disco restaurant. Poor man's cocaine, Klatsche always says.

He's not at home tonight, I can feel it. I know when he's there. Tonight, the flat next door is empty.

The barrister took the last train at around one. It was a nice try this evening, but we'd better not do that again. That dating shit just isn't for me. And nor is a man who takes the last train.

My phone makes a clicking sound.

Carla's texted me:

Are you up?

I call her.

'Hey,' she says.

'How are you?'

'Not too bad, what are you up to?'

'Smoking,' I say. 'How about you?'

'Cleaning windows.'

Carla always cleans her windows at night. She says it works better that way. Apparently, you don't get streaks because the sun doesn't shine at night.

I have no idea about that kind of thing.

'Why are you still up?' Carla asks.

'I was out with a barrister,' I say, 'in a restaurant. And it was so weird.'

'What was so weird, the barrister?'

'No,' I say, 'the barrister's OK. The problem was with the restaurant.'

I light another cigarette.

'Why, wasn't the food good?'

'It's too complicated to explain over the phone.'

I'm not in the mood for talking. I just wanted to listen.

'Come round tomorrow morning?' she asks.

'Sure,' I say.

'Get some sleep now then, OK?'

'One last cigarette,' I say.

'One last window,' she says.

I have to laugh.

'*Good night and good luck*,' she says in English.

'Same to you,' I say.

I smoke my cigarette to the end, go to bed and wait for my alarm clock to go off.

Black pudding

4kg marbled pork
1kg skin
1kg liver
200g salt
25g pepper
15g ground cloves
15g marjoram
15g thyme
10g caraway
10g cinnamon
Fresh blood

Boil the meat and skin, but don't let them get too soft.
Finely dice them, along with the liver.
Add the salt, spices and blood.
Stir well and then fill the pork intestines with the mixture.
Simmer for fifty to sixty minutes.

LIVES IN THE HAFENCITY AND HATES IT

On the dot of midday, I take off my court robe. You ironed old thing, I think, almost affectionately. Then I lock away the files, pocket my cigarettes and my phone and head over to Carla's. We're resuming at two, so there's time for a quick lunch between the victims' testimonies. Things are going badly for the three kidnappers. The stuff that's coming out is highly unpleasant. The guys evidently kept on trying to sell the girls on the internet as household slaves. But it didn't work because the wares were too battered. I'm looking forward to the last day of the trial, when the gentlemen get sent down. Maybe I'll run along after the prison van, whooping a bit.

It was nice to speak to Carla last night, for a few minutes it was like the old days, before those arseholes dragged her into the cellar. Her voice, her words, my easily excited yet seriously cool friend. The bitter, broken-down tone of the last few days wasn't there.

I light a cigarette and kick an empty Coke can down

the pavement. I've got a headache and the clatter of the can on the asphalt is kind of taking my mind off it. It was stupid not to have got more sleep. I never learn. When I'm lying in bed awake like that, I always think that at this point, it won't make much of a difference whether or not I get three hours' sleep. But the next day, it's clear that three hours' sleep would have been bloody useful.

I need to watch where I'm going while I kick this can. I almost got knocked down by a bus just now, at the Bismarck memorial.

It's full to bursting at Carla's. She's just taking two toasted sandwiches to a table. She blows me a kiss in passing, says, 'Hello sweetie.'

I sit at the bar.

Once Carla's come back round behind it, she pulls two beers at once and asks, 'Want a cheese toastie too?'

'No thanks,' I say, 'I'd rather have a croissant and two shots of coffee with milk and a lot of sugar.'

'Didn't you get any sleep last night?'

I shrug my shoulders.

'You're an idiot,' she says, carrying the beers away and then coming back to make me my coffee.

'So how was yesterday evening?'

'The barrister dragged me off to the dickhead restaurant in the old factory.'

'That red-brick dump on the main road with the name I can never remember?'

'That's the one,' I say.

'And?'

'It was wild. Sensational food, but everything else was fucking hideous. All the people at every table were hideous, and the tables themselves were hideous, and so were the lamps and the waiter and absolutely everything else. Dire. Except for the food, which was ferociously good. I just couldn't get my head around it, how that went together.'

'I see,' she says, pouring thick, dark coffee into a latte glass, adding a slug of steaming milk, shaking in a mountain of sugar and stirring it all up with a long spoon. 'Now I see.'

'What do you see?' I ask.

'I sometimes get this woman sitting here at the bar,' she says, 'you might know her by sight, a thin blonde, her hair always tied back really tight.'

'Don't think so,' I say.

'Doesn't matter,' says Carla, 'either way, she's a chef at that place. I think she might even be the head chef. She sits here in the afternoons before she opens up the kitchen and we have a bit of a chat. And although she never says so in so many words, I always get the feeling that she feels pretty shit about her life. Lives in the Hafencity and hates it. Makes good money in the fancy restaurant and hates it. Makes even more money from a TV cooking show and hates it. I think she kind of hates everything she does. She keeps saying that she envies me, and that it's so nice in my café, so cosy. And if I ever need a chef, to let her know. She'd do it for free and gratis, and all that. Then of course she always laughs and pretends she was only joking, but it's not a joke. She means it. And now that you tell me how awful that joint is, I get her a bit better. Although of course you have to ask yourself why she does all that if she hates it so much.'

'Can I have my sickly coffee please?'

'Oh, yeah, sure. Here.'

She puts one of the plump Portuguese croissants down in front of me too. My head stops aching on the spot.

'And the food was really that good?'

'Insanely good,' I say, 'there's no two ways about it. The woman can cook, bombshell, seriously.'

'Maybe I should take her up on her offer and get her grafting away in the kitchen here for free.'

She flits outside, new customers arriving on the pavement terrace.

I take the croissant, rip it in half through the middle, dip it in my coffee and shove it into my mouth. Relief.

'Why were you out with that barrister anyway?'

Carla puts a tray of dirty cups and ashtrays down behind the bar.

'Because he asked me,' I say, swallowing.

'You never go out with men who ask you to go out with them.'

'I've always liked the barrister,' I say.

Carla looks blankly at me, raises her hands and lifts her shoulders up high. 'So?'

I take a big swig of coffee and say: 'Klatsche brought this girl home the other night.'

'He didn't,' she says.

'I saw her,' I say.

'What did you see?'

'A girl, at his place, through the window. I was down in the street.'

'It was nothing,' says Carla.

'How do you know?'

'He told me so.'

'Oh, right,' I say. 'You two are best buddies at the moment, I'd almost forgotten. So obviously that means you chat about his latest fling, got it.'

'Whoa,' she says, 'where did that come from? You're acting so weird lately. And there was me thinking Klatsche was being over-sensitive.'

Maybe I should just stand up and leave.

Carla comes around the bar and puts her hand on my shoulder.

'Now, you listen to me. Klatsche's not in a good place. He doesn't have it easy with you. He loves you.'

I flinch back a little.

'You've got to stick this out for once, and that's that,' she says. 'You always put up so many barriers. The only way through to you is by chance. By accident. You know that. And Klatsche can handle a lot, seriously, but sometimes it drives him crazy that you're the way you are. The thing is, he thinks you're going to leave him any day. That you've had enough of him. He really doesn't know what to do.'

'I don't know what to do either.'

'You don't have to do anything. Just stop constantly refusing to accept that you like him.'

I take a sip of coffee and tear a big lump off my croissant.

'Or at least stop refusing to accept that he likes you,' she says. 'That he loves you, you silly cow.'

Love. I don't know.

'So what was up with that girl?' I ask.

'She's a waitress from a roller disco in Horn,' says Carla. 'She adores him. She turned up on his doorstep out of the blue. He wanted to be kind, so he had a drink with her. Then he drove her home.'

I shove baked pastry into my mouth.

'And we talked about it because I talked about Rocco with him,' Carla says.

'What about Rocco?' I ask, chewing.

'I'm glad he's back,' she says.

'I'm glad he's back too,' I say.

'But I'm a bit more glad,' she says.

'Oh,' I say. 'Seriously?'

'I think so,' she says.

'You remember what you've been through, right?'

She nods. 'But there you are,' she says, 'and this is the difference between us. Even so, I still want to let Rocco get close to me.'

I drink up my coffee and say, 'I have to get back to court.'

'Give it my love,' she says, smiling at me. 'What are you doing at the moment anyway?'

'Giving arseholes a thrashing.'

'Very good,' she says. 'And apart from that?'

'We've got a nasty case on,' I say, 'involves dissection. I think you'd rather not know.'

'Dissection,' she says, 'yeah, let's not go there.'

We have a quick hug, and that does me genuine good.

Somehow, I can manage that with Carla, better than anyone else. I'm almost outside when I remember something.

'Oh, Carla?'

'Yeah?'

'When's this chef woman's show on?'

'This evening,' she says, 'at ten.'

GREETINGS FROM HAMBURG-SAIGON

The sky is neither blue nor grey, it's got that toxic-yellow tinge. It's coming from the Elbe, a Saigon feeling, damp and heavy and sticky. There's always something of a relief about it, because even if you wanted to make an effort, you couldn't, it wouldn't work, it would be physically impossible. The water in your body isn't playing, it's on the ropes, the most you can do is saunter. And that idea is very popular in St Pauli at the best of times. Simply cocking up the day, entirely at your own pace.

It's barely five hundred metres from the court to the Kiez, but it takes me a good half hour to get there. And by the time I reach Millerntorplatz and look very slowly down the Reeperbahn, I'm really not in the mood to walk down the Mile. So I turn off at the Imperial Theater, which always looks a bit like it's dropped out of the redlight district, and head down Seilerstrasse. I drag my feet as I cross at the junction with Detlev-Bremer-Strasse, and there, on the corner, there's this pub, which is so dark that you can never even guess at what's going on in there. The only thing I'm certain of is that they serve a schnapps called Fuck, which costs a euro. Next door, someone's written *Shut your gob, Germany* on the wall with a fat marker pen.

I undo the top buttons on my shirt. The sky looms closer, it's a deep yellow now. I cross the road, sit in the shady gateway to the old school, light a cigarette and watch the show at the Hells Angel cobbler's – he's this beardy, hairy guy who looks as though he'll only resole shoes that he likes. As always, he's sitting behind his workbench, smoking and glaring, while a couple of biker babes lounge around on their motorbikes outside his shop. You rarely see customers at the Hells Angel cobbler's. Which is probably something to do with the fact that the man doesn't look as though you could either give him a job or ask him for a favour. The Hells Angel cobbler looks as though you should bring him a sacrifice, preferably a living one. To be a customer here takes balls in your trousers. And cash in your pocket. Over his workbench there's a sign, in big black letters: *In God We Trust. All Others Pay Cash.* But, in the end, that's all just for show. The moment the Hells Angel cobbler opens his mouth, a friendly smile and a velvety voice drop out. That's St Pauli for you. Hard on the outside, soft on the inside, and top-notch professionalism.

The Elvis hairdresser at the other end of the street operates along similar lines. Never go sucking up to your clientele – that's beneath your dignity. I like it there. Of course that has a bit to do with the thorough and consistent Elvis worship. The place is more of a shrine than a salon. But it's also because she just does whatever she thinks is right.

I drop my cigarette and skulk on down the street.

Sudden shouting. A woman's voice.

'Romy! ROMY!'

A little girl shoots out of the Kiez kindergarten, she races through the open gate, then across the street without looking right and left, and between two parked cars, then she darts off to the left and runs straight into my arms. I grab the kid and hold her tight. She's maybe four years old, she's got long, dark-blonde hair, which falls uncombed to her shoulders, she's wearing a dark-blue T-shirt and tatty jeans. Her legs are long and thin, her hips seem kind of bony, her jeans slipped down a bit on her sprint. She gives me a very serious look and breathes hard.

'Never do that again,' I say.

'Leave me alone.'

She's missing a front tooth.

'Never do that again,' I repeat. 'That's dangerous.'

She gives me a dirty look and presses her lips together.

'Romy.'

A young woman comes running over the street.

'Same old, same old,' she says.

She strokes Romy's head, takes her by the hand and leads her back to the kindergarten. The kid doesn't protest but, in the middle of the road, she turns back one last time and looks at me.

I wonder if she sensed it. If children actually pick up on looking similar to grown-ups. Standing there, face to face with the truculent Romy, it felt like looking at one of the pictures my dad took of me when I was little. Eyes, hair, jeans – I always looked like that too. Defiant, flying solo, bite me. I don't know if I was like that before my mother left Dad and me. I hardly know anything about the time before she went. My dad never liked to talk about it. And I can only remember two situations involving my mother – I was only two when she left. But I do remember standing in a cold, tiled stairwell. That must have been in Hanau, in the block of flats where we were living back then. My mother was holding me in her arms, and she kept pointing at all the light fittings and saying 'Lamp. Light.'

That's the nice memory.

The other goes like this: my dad doesn't stop crying for days. I keep quiet, sit at his feet and realise, little by little, that she isn't there anymore.

Sometimes, I seriously wonder how my mother is. I

know that she's on her third marriage now. The one to my dad's colleague, the guy she ran off to the US with, didn't last long. Now she's a dentist's wife and lives in Richmond, Wisconsin. I don't think she's happy. She sends me a card every year on my birthday. Considering how often I moved, I don't even know how she managed it before I washed up in St Pauli over ten years ago. I bet her bloke isn't even a tooth botherer really, he's probably in the CIA.

I turn and walk back towards the post office on Detlev-Bremer-Strasse. I buy a joke postcard from the souvenir shop on the corner. The postcard is of Paris. Underneath the Arc de Triomphe, it says *Millerntor*. I venture into the Hells Angel cobbler's and borrow a pen. I write my mother's address on the card. She puts it on every card she sends me, so I know it by heart. When I give the Hells Angel cobbler his pen back, he looks as though he's about to bite me, but he can't help that.

It's ten to five, the post office is still open. I walk in and join the queue. There are two women ahead of me. One is very young, she's got an ironclad Victoria Beckham pixie cut on her head, purple satin strappy sandals on her feet and a little Louis Vuitton bag in her hand. The other woman is early sixties or thereabouts, she's tall and hefty, and her dull ash-blonde hair hasn't seen a shampoo bottle for ages. Dry shampoo possibly. Her hair looks like a loofah. She's got a dog with her, a tiny Yorkshire terrier that could easily live in her hair and looks like a Christmas cracker in the woman's arms. In any other district of Hamburg, the dog would be sitting in the Beckham woman's handbag.

When it's my turn, I push my card over the counter.

'Airmail, please,' I say.

'Don't you want to write it?'

'What?'

'Don't you want to write it?'

The post-office man behind the counter is right. I should write something on it. But I have no idea what. He holds a biro out to me.

'What do other people write on their postcards?' I ask.

The counter guy is not in the mood for my stunt here. There are another five people behind me. He wants to close up.

'OK,' I say, 'give me a moment, yeah?'

Then I write: *Best regards from C.*

CLEAN TOOLS

I've just reached our building when my mobile rings. It's Calabretta.

'Is this a bad time?'

'Not at all,' I say. 'I was about to call you, actually. How's it looking?'

'We're turning the city upside down,' he says, 'but we're not getting anywhere. None of our guys has spotted anything at any of the hospitals or butchers' that we could latch on to. We've checked again in case we missed any link between the three dead men. Nothing. And none of any of their contacts has any kind of motive. The only possible candidate would be the young woman who accused Hendrik von Lell of sexual assault last year. For a moment I thought she might have taken things into her own hands, seeing as the guy got away with it. But she and her boyfriend emigrated to Melbourne four months ago. And anyway, why should she have knocked off the other two?'

'And we still have no trace of our first two victims' bodies?'

'Nothing,' he says. '*Lupara bianca*.'

'Bianca who?'

'Old mafia thing. Means "white sawn-off shotgun". Murder without a corpse. Bodies encased in concrete at some building site, or fed to the pigs.'

He sounds wooden as he says that.

'So what now?' I ask. 'Where do we go from here?'

He doesn't reply, just clears his throat.

'Should we maybe speak to Faller?'

I don't like asking, I don't want Calabretta to feel like I don't think he's up to it.

'I was hoping you'd suggest that, boss,' he says. 'When?'

'He's probably gone home by now,' I say. 'And he always spends Saturdays out with his daughter. We can't get much going over the weekend anyway. Sunday?'

'Sunday,' he says, then hangs up.

I open the door, climb the stairs to my flat, unlock my front door, close the door behind me, undress, run luke-warm water and lie in the bath. Hello Saigon, Riley here.

When I wake up, I'm freezing. Falling asleep in the bathtub is not a good trick. I get out, dry off and pull on a clean T-shirt and some boxer shorts. It's nearly ten. I walk into the kitchen, pull two bottles of beer out of the fridge, take my cigarettes and go over to Klatsche's.

I knock, he opens the door and says: 'Hey, baby.'

He's leaning in the doorway, six foot three, wearing a

dirty vest and ripped jeans, his shaggy, dark-blond hair peeking out from under a baseball cap at the back of his neck, his green eyes sparkling; he smells of sand and sun. He looks like a bloody surfer.

'Been to the seaside?' I ask, pulling a bit of white shell out of his hair.

'Yep,' he says, 'just got back. Took today off.'

Now and then in the summer, Klatsche likes to leave his locksmithery to his so-called employees. Assorted layabouts that he knows from his burglary days, or from jail, who earn a bit on the side by opening doors for him. Only at the customer's express request of course, says Klatsche. But I'm not sure he knows exactly who he's lending his nice clean tools to.

'How about you?' he asks. 'What have you been up to today?'

'Court,' I say.

'Why d'you keep hanging around that place?'

He puts his right hand around my waist and pulls me to him.

'I brought us something to drink.'

I hold up the beer bottles.

'You brought yourself, and that's what counts,' he says.

'Can I watch TV?' I ask.

'Sure,' he says, letting me go. 'What d'you want to watch?'

'A cooking programme,' I say.

She was walking down the road, had just been to the shops. She was wearing a bright dress and had a basket on her arm. It was summer, a lovely afternoon. Two young men came towards her, in shirts and suits, looking very dapper.

She didn't expect them to block her way.

She was irritated, but acted like it didn't bother her, and just went round to their left, she didn't want to let two idiots ruin her day, and at that moment, one of them said: What ugly tits.

NOTHING, WHY

I bump into them on Silbersackstrasse and they pull funny faces like they're two teenagers who've been getting up to mischief and then suddenly, Mum's standing in their bedroom.

'Hey,' I say.

'Hey,' says Carla. She gives me a kiss on the cheek and stands there biting her bottom lip.

'Where are you off to?' asks Rocco.

He's looking good in his old black shirt and tatty suit trousers.

'Elbe,' I say. 'What about you?'

'Er,' says Carla.

'Oh, just hanging around,' says Rocco, a bit too hastily.

'You're hanging around?'

'Yeah,' says Carla, 'out for a stroll, you know.'

'Uh-huh,' I say.

The door to the Silbersack opens and Dieter Korn walks out, slightly sweaty, clothes too tight, bald spot glistening, blue-tinted glasses too. He's not stupid enough to speak to Carla and Rocco in the middle of the street in broad daylight, but he looks over to them for a second, and it's immediately clear that the three of them know each other. And that Bonnie and Clyde here were probably just with him.

'What are you two getting up to with Karate Diddi?' I ask.

'Nothing, why?' says Rocco.

'Nothing at all,' says Carla.

'Rocco,' I say, pushing my sunglasses up into my hair, 'you're welcome to do business with anyone you like, but don't you drag my friend into it, OK? You've practically got one foot back in jail there, boy.'

'Chastity,' says Carla, 'calm the fuck down. Rocco was only helping me.'

'With what?' I ask. 'Are you wheeling and dealing here on the Kiez too these days?'

'I got myself a gun,' she says.

'Are you mad?'

'No ammo,' she says. 'I don't want to shoot the thing.'

'Then what *do* you want it for?' I ask.

'To defend myself,' she says. 'If anyone else ever tries to get up in my face, he'll be staring down the barrel.'

'You'll just be putting yourself in danger,' I say. 'What if he's got a gun too, but his happens to be loaded? You don't just go around pointing weapons at people, Carla.'

'You don't just go around dragging women into cellars and raping them.'

Right. You don't do that either.

'Did my colleagues ever get back to you about your case?' I ask.

'No,' she says. 'Nobody's got back to me. And I don't get the feeling that anybody ever will get back to me.'

'Bullshit, Carla,' I say, 'they're just busy.'

'Seriously, Chastity,' says Rocco, 'if Carla feels better with a piece in her handbag – why the hell shouldn't she have one?'

He's right. I've got something along those lines too. Not that I'm supposed to, any more than Carla is. I light a cigarette.

'OK. I don't know a thing about it.'

Carla smiles at me. 'I won't do anything stupid, don't worry.'

Rocco touches Carla's hand, and she slips hers into his. I drag on my cigarette and put my sunglasses back on.

'Come down to the Elbe with me?'

Carla takes my cigarette out of my mouth, drags on it, gives it back to me and says, 'Yeah, course we will.'

My phone rings. It's Klatsche.

LAMB-MINCE-BEER-KISS

He met me at four at the port. He said we needed to talk, not because we lay on his couch together yesterday evening watching a cooking programme, but despite that. He said that he's lost track, that he doesn't know where we're going anymore, but that he needs a direction. Because he's afraid that otherwise one day he'll end up lost. Unless we finally settle on a direction together.

When I was his age, shit like that would never even have occurred to me.

He keeps on surprising me.

I said that I'm not good at talking. That I've never been on any track and that any direction I've ever been going in has been accidental. And that in my life to date, I've only ever got lost when I've thought: Oh, OK, I'm here now.

'All right,' he said, 'if you don't want to talk to me, you'll have to walk with me. Until we've found a direction.'

It's seven o'clock by this point, the evening sun is flying through the city, the buildings are giving off their warmth to the streets between them, we've been walking for three hours now. We're not talking, we're not saying a word, we're just going for a walk. A few minutes ago, Klatsche took my hand.

There's a man and a woman sitting outside a snack bar on a corner. They're sitting on two upturned beer crates, they're probably around sixty, but they look like they're a hundred and ten. Each of them is holding a can of beer and they both look very content.

'Well then,' says the woman. 'We'll drink these up first, though, won't we?'

'Yes,' says the man. 'There's got to be time for that. We won't let them take that away from us.'

Klatsche stops, looks at me and says: 'Beer?'

'Yes,' I say, 'we won't let them take that away from us.'

He gets two cans of beer from the kiosk, then we walk on, hand in hand, accompanied by two cool blondes. We walk until it gets dark, on and on through our part of town, through two parks and back onto the streets and, because we end up properly thirsty, we go to the Twenty Flight Rock.

This is a men's pub. Which doesn't mean that there are no women here, quite the contrary. The women here are properly good. The ones here have guts. They wear pencil skirts with slits, low-cut blouses and shirts, and stockings with seams, and they never wear flat shoes. Their hair is perfect and hard-core, styled to take anything a night in a bar like this can throw at you. The men all wear jeans that look like the originals from 1873. They wear shirts like the ones Robert Mitchum and Johnny Cash used to wear, and professionally cleaned leather shoes. Every note of music from the speakers is by people who are already dead, with the sole exception of Jon Spencer and his Blues Explosion.

We sit at the bar and each of us drinks three beers, then we walk on a bit further, we walk down to the port and wave goodbye to a cargo ship, we walk back to the Kiez and end up in the Rakete. It's after midnight and the dancing's just starting in the Rakete. I don't actually dance, but Klatsche's invented a dance that works. He puts his right arm around my waist and then we move at half speed, or quarter speed if the music is very fast. That way, you never get into too much of a state, and you can even drink and smoke at the same time.

The boss at the Rakete still DJs in person every Saturday. The boss has the best brilliantined hair in the city and most of his music comes from Detroit. So we dance. We dance for two, three hours, I don't know for certain, but it's still dark as we tumble out of the Rakete and these days it doesn't start getting light till about four. Klatsche's hungry, so we stop off at a kebab shop on the way home.

We're still not talking.

Klatsche orders a beer and lamb meatballs, I order a beer and a raki. We fetch our own beers from the huge fridge, the lamb and the raki are brought over.

'So?' I ask.

He smiles at me and takes my hand. 'So what?'

'Is there a direction lying around here anywhere?'

'Can you see one?'

He's not going to be lured out of his reserve, he's clearly insisting that I go first.

'I like walking the city with you,' I say.

'Sorry? I didn't quite catch that.'

I take a deep breath.

'I like being with you,' I say, and because I want to speak loudly enough this time, I say it a bit too loudly, and the people at the other tables turn to look at us. Klatsche doesn't say a thing, he just grins, leans against the wall and looks at me. I try to hold his gaze and down my raki. He's still not saying anything and now the whole joint is extremely interested in what's going on between us. Please, I think, please let something happen, anyone. I hastily count to ten to stop myself from running straight back out onto the street. On seven, the doner spit tips out of its stand. The man whose job it is to hack at the meat just about saves himself by leaping into the salad buffet. He fires a curse up at the heavens, then all the men behind the counter start swearing, it's total chaos.

Klatsche's still grinning at me.

'So, Riley,' he says, 'make you jump?'

'No,' I say, 'you?'

He shakes his head, sticks a bit of meatball in his mouth, chews, chases it down with a swig of beer, then he pushes his food and my beer aside, leans over the table, grabs me with both hands on the back of my neck and gives me a big, fat, lamb-mince-beer-kiss.

'Henri Klassman,' I say, 'you're revolting.'

'Don't call me Henri Klassman,' he says.

'It's your name.'

'But you know that's no business of anybody here.'

He kisses me again; we drink up our beer and go home. The kebab men have fixed the doner spit now.

The shop's operational again.

She was standing on an escalator, the escalator was going up. She was daydreaming, not thinking about anything in particular. The hand that grabbed her from behind, up her skirt, gripped hard. It really hurt. She screamed at the guy as he hurriedly squeezed past her, she hurled insults at him, she was livid. He ran up the escalator and once he'd got to the top, he turned to her and said: What d'you want then, you slag. C'mere then, you slag. I'll knife you, you slag.

She started to feel afraid of him and tried to somehow go back down the escalator, she didn't want to walk past the man.

None of the other men on the escalator helped her. None so much as uttered a word. Some wouldn't even let her past.

COMMERCIAL BREAK

We're sitting in Klatsche's living room, on the window sill, in the sun with the window open, we're dangling our legs, we're drinking warm, sugary coffee and watching the Sunday morning on our street.

'Ad break,' I say.

'Total ad break,' says Klatsche. He's got his arm around my shoulders.

This morning, our road really does seem tailor-made for a cheery coffee advert. Peaceful with exactly the right shot of life. If I were a coffee-company boss, I'd snap it up. I'd put a few bars of TV-friendly guitar music in the background and then I'd broadcast it uncut.

The sun's high above the rooftops at this time of day, and it's pouring the perfect light onto the scene. The ice-cream parlour guy is setting out his round ice-cream parlour tables and multicoloured chairs, he's pulling tub after tub of his freshly churned ice cream from the freezer. Then he drinks a strong, dark coffee.

The beautiful guy from the upcycled design shop is

getting out of his old VW bus, all saltwater curls, behind him, one, two, three, his girlfriend's kids jump out of the open side door, his girlfriend climbs down after them, her long, dark curls look like springs. All five of them are getting back from the Baltic. They often do that, just drive to the beach for the night and sleep out under the stars. He opens up the shop. Not to sell anything, no. The only reason they open on Sundays is to have breakfast on the bench outside the shop. The other beautiful guy from the upcycled design shop is here now too. He's still kind of bleary-eyed, he often stays out dancing until late, I've heard that he's pretty good. And then there are two young women who must have slept at the shop, for whatever reason. They all sit down together on the homemade wooden bench outside the upcycled design shop, drinking milky coffee out of tall glasses. From their faces, you'd think it was cocoa.

There are a few solitary souls hanging around outside the Kandie Shop. Early risers, like the guy in the elegant shirt who smokes thin cigarillos and is proudly watching over his old Opel Senator. And the DJ who's up at eight the same as ever despite playing a set last night, either because his kids are visiting or because he likes it that way. And the gallery owner who's already had to take his dog out, by which point you might as well stay out and read the paper in peace, seeing as it's so mellow on this street today for a change. All three of them are drinking coffee. The DJ has a double espresso, the Opel Senator man's got an americano and the gallery guy has a cappuccino.

In a sunny parking spot in the middle of the street, Rocco Malutki is tinkering with an old Schwalbe scooter. The Schwalbe is ochre yellow, and on the back-left mudguard, there's a picture of a stallion in the sunset.

'Hey, look,' I say, 'there's Rocco.'

Each of us sips from our coffee cups. How lucky that we're up here on the fourth floor, nobody can see us from below, we're well out of the whole advert thing.

'How's that nutter got hold of a Schwalbe already?' I ask. 'He's only been back in town a day or two.'

'He wangled it,' says Klatsche.

Wangled it. Right.

'What d'you think about Rocco and Carla?' I ask.

He finishes his coffee and whispers in my ear. 'Perfect.'

I push him away and look at him. Then I look up into the Hamburg sky, then down onto our picture-book street, and then something very weird happens.

OFFICER IN CHEF'S CLOTHING

Klatsche and Rocco are tinkering like crazy with the old Schwalbe. It's hard to get the thing to start. After two hours, I'm no longer in the mood to watch. Eventually, drinking coffee in the street gets old. I set off for Carla's, to drink coffee there.

Carla's standing in the kitchen, stirring a rose-pink liquid in a large jug.

'Raspberry lemonade,' she says.

She throws a few ice cubes and a handful of flowers into the jug.

'What are the flowers for?' I ask.

'Tastes more colourful.'

We go round the front into the café. Not very busy today, everyone must be at the beach. Carla takes two large glasses off the shelf and pours us some lemonade. OK, lemonade then. I sit at the bar, she stands behind it and starts washing dishes.

'How's the gun?' I ask.

'It's fine,' she says.

'Do you have it on you the whole time?'

'That's why I bought it.'

'And? Do you feel better?'

She breaks off from washing up.

'No,' she says. 'I don't feel better. I feel shit. I'm scared, no matter where I am. I'm scared in my bed, I'm scared in my bathroom, I'm scared here in the café, I'm scared on the street. I'm scared when I'm alone and I'm scared when I'm not alone. I'm even scared when you're with me. My entire being consists of ninety per cent fear. And the rest is a mixture of nausea and rage.'

'Carla,' I say.

'You can't help me,' she says. 'Nobody can help me.'

'I'd been hoping that you've been doing a tiny bit better in the last few days.'

'I'm trying to be brave,' she says. 'I won't let them get me down. But those arseholes...'

She carries on with the washing up and breaks the handle off a cup. She takes a deep breath and looks at me. There are tears in her eyes.

'Cigarette?' I ask.

'Yes,' she says.

We go outside, sit on the pavement and smoke, I've got my arm around her and she's telling me about Rocco Malutki. Although in comparison with Carla's usual experiences with men, there's not much to tell. There's no boozing, there are no wild nights, no dramas. There's only been one cautious snog with a portside view, under a plastic palm tree.

Since then, they've seen each other every day.

He just pops into the café, sometime in the afternoon. When Carla closes up in the evening, they go for a walk or for something to eat. And when Carla gets tired, he takes her home. Yesterday evening, she didn't want to be alone. So he stayed the night. He waited till she fell asleep, then he withdrew to the living room.

'Sounds good,' I say.

She nods.

'And it's not true that I'm always scared.'

She drags on her cigarette.

'When Rocco's with me, I sometimes forget.'

I pick up a bit of gravel from the street and let it trickle through my fingers.

'I made up with Klatsche,' I say.

Carla holds up her glass. 'I'll drink to that,' she says.

'Cheers.'

We smoke our cigarettes, finish our drinks and go back in. I sit at the bar a while longer and flick through the Sunday paper, and then suddenly there's this woman sitting beside me, I didn't even notice her come in. She's almost as tall as me and because she's wearing a vest top, you can see that she's in extremely good shape. She has smooth, Hanseatic-blonde highlighted hair, tied back in a severe bun at the nape of her heck. She's sitting next to me, reading yesterday's paper and drinking one of Carla's homemade lemonades. I think that one's apple. I recognise the woman from somewhere. Carla smiles at her as she walks past.

Ah. Now I remember. The chef.

I watched her programme. I didn't catch exactly what it was about because Klatsche spent the whole time giving me tight little sideways glances, which ended up really irritating me, but I did make a note of her face. Mainly because of the food, of course, that she's clearly capable of cooking, but also because she looks seriously brisk. Like a military officer in chef's clothing. That struck me when I saw her on TV on Friday, but she's even more intense in real life. She has the air of being born to give orders. I try to focus on my paper again.

'Are you OK, Carla?'

The chef's stopped reading and has turned to Carla.

Carla looks at her and shrugs. 'Not too bad,' she says. She takes a cloth and wipes it over the bar. 'No cause for concern.'

The chef isn't buying it, I can tell.

'Well, anyway, I'm glad your café is open again,' she says.

Carla just smiles and doesn't reply. The chef smiles back and sips at her lemonade. She's clocked that Carla doesn't want to talk about it. And she's noticed that I'm weighing her up. She turns her head and looks at me.

'Is there a problem?'

Oh. Awkward. But Carla's on the ball, as always when I'm out of line, and before I can start to make an idiot of myself, apologising constantly, she steps in and says: 'Jules, this is my friend Chastity Riley, I told her about you, she's a big fan of the food at Taste.'

She adds a beaming smile, and at once a subtle but friendly link has been created between the chef and me. The woman holds out her hand.

'Jules Thomsen. Pleased to meet you.'

'Hi,' I say. 'Chastity Riley.'

She's got a handshake like a carpenter.

'What did you have?'

'The fish,' I say, 'the one with all the herbs. It was great.'

'Ah, yes,' she says with a nod. 'My sous chef looks after that these days. I've almost completely given up the fish section.'

'So you don't feel like doing fish anymore?' I ask, which makes me feel like Reinhold Beckmann or someone, interviewing her on TV.

'Sure,' she says, 'but I think you have to focus on one thing. And I chose meat.'

'Doesn't that get boring? Nothing but meat?' I ask. Asking people about how they feel makes *me* feel more like Reinhold Beckmann than ever.

'Not at all,' she says. 'I've got seven sausage dishes alone on the menu at the moment, and each of them is an adventure, the herbs, the spicing...'

Just now, she seemed so fierce. Now, talking about cooking, she's softening.

'The man I was with had that Italian sausage,' I say.

'The salsiccia with fried potatoes?' she asks.

'That's the one,' I say. 'He went practically out of his mind. He said he'd never tasted anything like that salsiccia in his life.'

'What kind of guy was he, your companion?'

'A barrister,' I say, 'why do you ask?'

'I'm interested in the people I cook for. Come on, describe him. I'd really appreciate it.'

'OK,' I say. 'He's tall and rather thin, and he always wears a suit. He's clever, he's got a sense of humour, he doesn't have much money but he does have a soft spot for the underdog. I think he's a decent human being.'

'OK.' She seems confused. 'That's rare.'

She pokes around in her nearly empty lemonade glass.

'What's rare?' I ask.

'Nice men at Taste,' she says.

I got that feeling too.

'I got that feeling too,' I say.

'Another drink, you two?'

Carla flits past, the place has actually filled up now.

I shake my head.

'No, thank you,' says Jules Thomsen.

She fishes a packet of cigarettes out of her bag. 'Do you smoke?'

'Of course,' I say.

We slip down from our bar stools, sit at a table outside the door and smoke. The chef stares at her cigarette.

'Are you and Carla good friends?'

'We're like family,' I say.

'What happened?' she asks.

She looks at me. She clearly knows that *something* happened. She's not stupid and she likes Carla. I don't want to play games with her, but I don't want to go behind Carla's back either, so I don't answer.

'Was it what I think it was?' she asks.

'I don't know what you think it was,' I say.

'Somebody hurt her,' she says. 'It was brutal, you can tell. It's like there are cracks in her eyes.'

I drag on my cigarette. I think that's an answer.

'I wish,' she says, 'that one day, guys like that would get to feel for themselves the fear they cause people. Just once, just one fucking time. I bet they'd shit themselves. Maybe they'd even die of fear. Is that a thing? Can you die of fear?'

GUT FEELINGS

Calabretta is waiting for me by the old bunker on the Baumwall. When he sees me coming, he pushes his sunglasses up into his hair. His eyes are tiny. I don't think there's been a minute in the day until now when he hasn't had the sunglasses on. He looks tired.

'*Moin*,' I say.

'*Moin*.'

'Everything OK with you?'

He sticks out his chin and turns his mouth down, he starts moving, glances vaguely left and right, and marches through the red light, me stumbling behind him. He's setting a brisk pace.

'What's wrong?' I ask – we're almost at the Kehrwiederspitze already. 'Bad night's sleep?'

'No sleep at all,' he says.

'Why's that?'

'Pulled two all-nighters in a row. In the Kiez and the Schanzenviertel.'

I didn't know he still painted the town such a bright

red. I always thought he was different from me. I thought he was more grown up.

'New girlfriend or what?'

'Don't be daft,' he says. 'When did I last have a girl-friend?'

True. He doesn't have much luck with women. Presumably the usual cop's disease – too much work, the work's too hard, too unpredictable. He's not up for that.

'There's some kind of angel of death out there,' he says, 'there could be some woman running through the night, killing men. And we still have no idea where to start. It's driving me nuts.'

'What makes you think it's a woman?'

'We've got that hair we found on Dejan Pantelic's head,' he says. 'And my gut tells me so.'

His gut. I don't know.

'I prowled around all the nightlife hotspots,' he says, 'I went into every shitting pub, every club. I was hoping that some*thing* or some*one* would catch my eye.'

'And?'

'Nothing, it's sickening.'

I haven't a clue either, I think, but it's kind of weird that I really couldn't give a shit. The fact that we've got nothing to show for our investigations bothers me just as little as the fact that three men have died.

I can't explain it, it's not like me. Whatever. Either way, I really ought to pull my socks up. We need a result or two fairly soon. The chief prosecutor's starting to get twitchy, and so is the press. They've been milking it for over a week and dishing up the most desperate shit. 'Bone Saw Massacre'. 'Body Snatchers'. 'Hamburg, City of Floaters'.

Calabretta walks through the Speicherstadt as if he'd got a dynamo up his arse. He wants to see Faller.

'Sorry,' I say.

'What for?'

'For not being any help.'

'It's not your job to help me,' he says. 'It's enough for you to give me orders. You're my boss. You're in charge of this business. Aren't you?'

Calabretta's not just tired, he's pissed off with me.

'It might not be my job,' I say, 'but I still think it's my duty. That's how it was with Faller, and that's how it's always been between us before. Could we slow down a bit please?'

'Oh. Yeah. Sure.'

He slams on the brake and sounds gentler again. He's such a nice guy, he can't even get properly pissed off.

'Don't beat yourself up about it.'

'But I am beating myself up about it,' I say, 'and I don't

know why I'm not firing on all cylinders with this business. Let's be honest: it's a sexy case. I ought to be out and about with you day and night.'

'But?' asks Calabretta.

'I can't be arsed,' I say.

'Why not? Innocent people have been killed. You're the fanatic for justice out of the two of us.'

'Exactly,' I say.

He stops and looks at me. 'Exactly? What?'

'I get the feeling,' I say, 'that they weren't innocent.'

'Oh, please,' says Calabretta. 'What the hell is that supposed to mean?'

I shrug my shoulders. 'It's just a feeling.'

'Bollocks, Riley.'

That's what I love about him. He never treats me like his public prosecutor. He treats me the same way he'd treat any other idiot.

We walk on, I light myself a cigarette.

And it's not bollocks, I think. It's more than a feeling. I'm sure of it. Sure that the dead men weren't innocent. That's why I don't think it's a tragedy that they're dead. And I don't think Calabretta understands that.

'Oh yeah,' he says, 'how are our human traffickers getting on?'

'Tomorrow it's the summing-up,' I say. 'And then those

guys will hopefully be out of the picture for a few years. Anything else would be a fucking miracle.'

'Good work,' he says.

'You too.'

We walk past the Kaispeicher. The lighthouse is over that way. The only thing missing is Faller.

LOOKING LIKE A STONE OR THEN AGAIN, NOT

'A man without a belly is like the sky without stars, or so they say in Italy,' Calabretta had said, tapping the spare tyre above his belt, after which we decided to go to the Kleine Pause for currywurst and chips. The Kleine Pause is the kind of diner you normally only get on TV. Open almost round the clock, with a break between five and six in the morning and with regulars on shifts – there's always at least two of them there at any one time. The ladies behind the grill look amazing, each has her own brand. There's one, for instance, who's rocked the craziest hair colours over the years. Blue, purple, red, stripy, she's had them all. And so now we're sitting at the polished eighties-style bar, drinking draught Alsterwasser shandy and copping insults. Insults from the chefs are part of the Kleine Pause experience. If you behave yourself, the insults are friendly; if you can't behave, you get properly sworn at and thrown out. My suspicion is that they basically mean well by perpetually scolding their customers like this. As if the people here need lifelong upbringing, to keep them on the straight and narrow and stop them getting into trouble.

'We ordered currywurst and chips twice,' Calabretta says in the direction of the counter, holding up his finger.

It's taking too long for his liking.

'We'll see about that – the two of you aren't going to starve, my dumpling.'

Calabretta gulps down his Alsterwasser and tries not to take offence. He knows that it'll only result in more of the same.

'How was Naples, anyway?' I ask. 'You haven't really told me.'

'Lovely,' he says, and there's a strange glitter swimming in his eyes. It's not always there when Calabretta talks about Italy. That seems to kind of depend on his mood from day to day. There are days when Italy's nothing but a sordid dung heap, mafia-infested, corrupt, whiny. And there are days when Italy is the promised land, the lost homeland, the great longing. Today is clearly one of the sentimental days.

'Should we have gone for pizza?' I ask.

'We'd probably have been served sooner,' he says.

He acts grumpy and stares out of the window. Which is Calabretta for 'give me a second'.

Maybe exactly this is the gateway to true friendship.

When you learn to decipher the other person's codes.

By the time our food arrives, his eyes are dry. He can look at me again.

'I was only in Naples for three days,' he says, stabbing a lump of currywurst. 'I met up with a few friends there and then I spent the rest of the time with my family. I was only intending to go over for lunch. But I ended up staying.'

'Your family live near the volcano, don't they?'

He nods. 'In a little village. Where vines grow on people's rooftops and it smells of clam sauce, even in the morning.'

'Isn't that a bit dangerous?'

'What, the clam sauce?'

'No, living so close to Vesuvius.'

'If Vesuvius goes off, it tends to explode,' he says. 'By which point it makes no difference either way whether you're sitting in the crater or on a fancy terrace in Sorrento. If Vesuvius goes off, the whole coast will go up. That thing's dynamite, it's lethal.'

'Oh,' I say.

'But that's life,' he says. 'The most beautiful places are often the most dangerous.'

He shoves a mountain of chips in his mouth, chews and glances out of the window again. Outside, the wind's got up. The trees drop a few leaves in a lacklustre way. He looks back at me.

'I went to my uncle's grave for the first time in years. He was two years younger than I am now when they buried him. I hadn't expected it to floor me like that. That's why I had to stay on in the village, at my aunt's. Things can happen so fast, and suddenly you've got no family left.'

I know, my friend, I know.

'What did your uncle die of?' I ask.

'The Camorra,' he says. 'He was a carabiniere and he took his job seriously. They killed him. They shot him right outside San Domenico Maggiore and just left him there. Outside a church, you know? They used my dead uncle to send a message.'

He packs more chips into his mouth and follows up with a large piece of currywurst. He can hardly chew it all.

I always wondered why he was such a through-and-through cop, why he sometimes gets so obsessed, can never let a thing go. Now I know. And I think he tends towards comfort eating.

I push my plate away and move his aside, then I put my hands on his forearms and give them a squeeze.

'Another beer?'

He laughs and chews and nods, I let go of his arms, raise my hand and order two beers.

'Bloody drunkards,' says the redhead, whose hair was pink only last week.

'You know what,' says Calabretta, once he's finally swallowed down his huge lump of fast food, 'there's something in Naples that you should really go and see one day.'

'Genuinely?' I ask.

For the life of me, I have no idea what I should go anywhere to see.

'A chapel,' he says, 'not particularly spectacular, hard to find. And this chapel has the kind of marble Jesus you get in churches. After the cross – got that all over with – he's been taken down and now he's lying there. This Jesus is covered from head to foot with a shroud.'

A dead man made of stone with a shroud made of stone. Uh-huh. Doesn't sound like anything special in a church.

'Doesn't sound like anything special,' I say.

'Right,' he says. 'But the crazy thing is that even though I've seen that sculpture so often, every time I'm there, I have to touch it again. Because I just can't believe that the shroud is carved from marble. It's so fine and so light, it looks like it could just blow away. In all my life I've never seen stone that looked less like stone.'

'So?' I ask. 'What's that got to do with me?'

'You're the exact opposite,' he says. 'I've never met anyone who looks so much like stone but is anything but.

I swear, Riley, if people knew, they'd put you up on display too.'

I lean back and cross my arms over my chest.

'How about an ice cream?' he asks.

I kick him gently under the table, then we stand up, pay, hear that we're miserable layabouts, walk out of the door and round to the ice-cream parlour next door, where we each get two scoops of Amarena cherry and lie in the deck-chairs on the pavement.

Calabretta looks into the windy treetops above our heads. The wind's got up.

'So,' he says, 'what now?'

'With what?'

'With the dead men,' he says. 'Where do we go next? Faller wasn't much help.'

'Could there be something we haven't even thought of?' I ask. 'A completely different solution? A corner that our questions can't get into? Some kind of blind spot?'

Calabretta looks like he wants to say something, like there's something on the tip of his tongue, an idea, a start, anything. But then he crumples, breathes out and says: 'I'm so tired.'

There's a clatter beside me, a woman's coming down the three steps from the ice-cream parlour to the pavement. Her black curls look like they're very grey beneath the dye, and so does her face, but her hair is defiantly youthful in style, done up with a pink clip on the back of her head. She's wearing it with an asymmetrical white lace skirt, a wild-looking thing with proper jaggedy teeth at the hem. Her denim jacket is embroidered with heaps of sequins. Death's heads, flowers, hearts, tears. She's wearing bizarre canvas trainers that are, on the one hand, undoubtedly trainers but have, on the other hand, genuinely high, spindly heels. Stiletto plimsolls. But she can hardly walk, she's coming out of the ice-cream parlour on two crutches, she really needs a wheelchair. It takes me a moment to realise that her wheelchair's over the road. She's actually getting into that flash silver S-Class coupé that's been double-parked this whole time. Those are some serious pimp wheels, chrome this and alloy that, all the trimmings. Except that there's a huge ding rusting away on the back rear mudguard. The woman climbs awkwardly into her Merc and starts the engine. The motor sounds like a tank.

'Well, one thing's for certain,' I say, 'it wasn't her.'

When she came home in the evenings, the ugly little man who lived across the road would stand by his window, pull down his trousers and jerk himself off. He did it in the dark at first, then in the light and sooner or later, he was prancing around stark naked in the window. It was seriously getting on her nerves. She wanted some peace, and to be able to look out of the window again.

At some point, she called the police.

The woman from the vice squad came round right away. Watched it all very closely. She even saw the wanker in action, he probably thought two women were better than one.

I'm afraid I must advise you not to press charges, said the policewoman. He might get fined a few hundred euros, but nothing more. And he'd know who reported him. I wouldn't be able to guarantee your safety.

What should I do then? she asked.

Put up with it the best you can, said the policewoman, and maybe buy a whistle in case he does attack you.

BURN THE WHOLE PLACE DOWN

I'm standing in the courtroom, it's been a long, tough day, and bloody humid yet again, the defence have been trampling on my nerves with their cry-baby closing speeches, and now the judge is passing sentence, and I'm on the point of rioting. If those shitheads don't make total idiots of themselves in jail, they'll be back home by next Christmas, sitting around the tree.

Never in my life would I have dreamt that their bullshit defence would actually work.

First-time offenders with traumatic childhoods, my arse. Such terrible poverty. And it wasn't *organised* human trafficking, your honour, the lads are cousins. They were just helping each other out. You have to make a living somehow. I could puke.

And the two perpetrators standing between their lawyers, smirking at each other over their cushy sentences. If I were one of the victims, I'd burn the whole place down.

I have to get out of here.

Out on the street, I take a deep breath, smoke a cigarette

in three drags and turn my mobile back on. Five missed calls. One from Klatsche, four from Calabretta.

And a voicemail: 'Riley, call me back as soon as you can. We've got a lead. And it might actually go somewhere for a change.'

I call Calabretta, he answers right away.

'Hey,' I say, 'shoot.'

'This afternoon, a guy turned up at the station on Lerchenstrasse. Says that on the night Dejan Pantelic disappeared, he saw a woman kicking a man's head in. And the way he described the man, it could actually have been Pantelic.'

'Can he describe the woman?'

'He can.'

'Not bad,' I say. 'Why's the guy only just turned up now?'

'He's a bit of a freak,' he says. 'Schulle's giving him a grilling right now. Seems like the guy's been running around after this woman for weeks or even months. Seems like some kind of stalker. And he's probably shitting himself that we might have a problem with that.'

'Got it,' I say, waving down a taxi, 'see you shortly then.'

I'M SURE YOU ARE AWARE OF YOUR CURRENT LEGAL POSITION

'Where are they then?' I ask.

Calabretta's standing by the window in the corridor outside the interview rooms, smoking.

'Number five,' he says.

I knock on the second door on the left, count to three and walk in.

The guy's a little wiener, maybe in his early to mid-twenties. He's got buzzcut, dark, stubbly hair, his white scalp glinting through in several places. There are beads of sweat glittering on his spotty brow. He's wearing a black hooded T-shirt, cheap, thin jeans and shoes scuffed to grey. He's chewing on his bottom lip and doesn't look at me as I come in.

'This is Ms Riley,' says Schulle, 'the public prosecutor.'

Stubble-Head mutters something incomprehensible but does now glance over to me. He stares obtrusively at my shirt. He needs to watch himself. I'm in a bad mood – it's possible that I'll be overcome by the urgent need to give someone a slap.

'OK,' says Schulle, 'so, once again, you didn't just see the woman bring the man to the ground with a kick to the face, you also saw a second woman there. Have I got that straight?'

Stubble-Head slumps deeper in his chair, crosses his arms over his chest and says, 'When the guy stopped moving, she phoned someone. And then the other woman turned up. She arrived in a flash car.'

I sit on a chair in a dark corner and keep quiet.

'What kind of car was it?' asks Schulle.

'Saab estate.'

'Colour?'

'Dark.'

'And then what?'

'And then I went for a drink.'

'You can't be serious.'

'Can I have a fag?'

'This is a no-smoking area.'

'Can I go?'

We can't hold him. The spot of stalking we suspect him of is nothing like enough, nobody's even made a complaint. But Stubble-Head doesn't know that. And Schulle does what I'd do myself. He says: 'That depends.'

'On what?'

'Whether you'll lend us another half-hour of your valuable time,' says Schulle, 'and help our specialists put together a couple of photofits.'

'Why?'

'Because,' says Schulle, 'that means that I and my colleague here from the prosecution service will be so busy looking for the two women that we might just forget to start proceedings against you for stalking.'

He leans in towards him slightly and lowers his voice.

'I'm sure you are aware of your current legal position.'

Stubble-Head chews on his bottom lip again.

'OK,' he says.

'Excellent,' says Schulle with a smile, 'that's very wise of you.'

I stand up and make myself scarce. Calabretta is still standing by the window and smoking. I go over to him and light up myself.

'We've got more luck than brains,' I say.

He nods and drags deeply on his cigarette. 'In half an hour, max, we'll have two photofit images to put out, and we've finally got something to work with.'

That's something at least.

'Have you heard from Faller?' he asks. 'I've been worrying because he wasn't at the lighthouse yesterday evening.'

'No,' I say, 'I haven't. But I don't think there's anything up.'

I pull out my phone and call Faller. It rings six times and then his wife answers.

'Chastity Riley here,' I say, 'is your husband around?'

'He's in the garden,' she says. 'Pruning the roses.'

I put my hand over the phone and tell Calabretta: 'There is something up. He's pruning roses.'

Calabretta frowns.

'Do you want me to put my husband on for you?' asks Mrs Faller. She sounds a bit prickly. She seems mighty pleased that the stupid roses are finally getting pruned.

'No, no,' I say, 'it's not important.'

He'd been following her for a good thirty minutes. No matter which shops she went into, which street she turned down, he walked after her. He tagged along into the U-Bahn station, he got into the same carriage, he even changed trains with her. He just stuck to her heels, wouldn't stop.

At first it was just annoying, then it got creepy.

He was scaring her, partly because of the way he stared. Her heart was racing and she started to sweat.

But then there came a time when she was quicker than him, she got off the train while he was still on it.

Once the train had gone, she stood on the platform and burst into tears. She was furious.

Because yet again, she hadn't stood up for herself.

That arsehole had been allowed to scare her, just because he felt like it, and she hadn't stood up for herself. He'd had his fun, she'd got the shitty end of the stick. Next time, she swore to herself, she'd fight back.

Next time, she'd be prepared.

MAD AS HELL

The person on the screen has long curly hair and looks like a friendly version of Heidi Klum. A total everywoman face, utterly useless as a photofit.

'We can't do a thing with this,' I say.

'Quite,' says Calabretta, propping his head on his left hand.

'And then there's this,' says Schulle.

He opens another image. If it wasn't so awful, I'd laugh, because the second picture tells us about as much as a stick man. With a little imagination, you can tell that it's meant to be a woman. Calabretta groans.

'Sheesh. Can you please close that thing?'

Outside, we can hear Brückner swearing and kicking the coffee machine.

'The guy couldn't even really decide on the women's hair colour,' says Schulle. 'He reckoned one might have been blonde and the other too, but he couldn't say for certain. Maybe he didn't want to. I tried everything, seriously.'

'How about the description of the victim?' I ask.

'Better,' says Schulle. 'We showed him photos of Dejan Pantelic, and he said he could have been the man. So we're assuming that it was and hoping that that's true and that we haven't got a fourth victim lying around somewhere.'

'At least now we know that we're looking for two women,' I say. 'Don't let it get you down, OK?'

'Of course not,' says Calabretta. 'We've got some plain-clothes units out in the Kiez, they've been there since yesterday evening. Our witness was at least able to tell us with reasonable precision where he tended to follow the woman with the curls, which was always in the area between Simon-von-Utrecht-Strasse and Wohlers Allee. We've got the guys patrolling that whole area, tailing every woman who looks even remotely like the photofit. We're also still looking for links between the victims.'

I go over to the open window and light a cigarette.

'Our witness didn't happen to know where the woman lives or where she works, did he?' I ask.

'He swore blind that he didn't,' says Schulle.

Brückner's back in the room now, holding a cup of coffee and leaning against his desk.

'I went back to see Dejan Pantelic's girlfriend,' he says, 'and an ex of Jürgen Rost's. Didn't get anything new, apart from a feeling that Rost didn't have a great deal of respect for women. Just sounded that way, you know? Kind of the way she talked about him. And we know that Pantelic lashed out now and then.'

'Hendrik van Lell was charged with sexual assault,' I say.

'Bingo,' says Brückner.

'OK, men,' says Calabretta, 'I want every ex-girlfriend, lover or mere acquaintance of all three victims. Go through everyone they ever met. There must be a woman in common.'

'And she,' I say, 'must have some reason to be mad as hell with all three of them.'

THE CELLAR SITUATION

I ought to like what I'm seeing. Carla's standing behind the bar in her café, getting two glasses of white wine ready for Klatsche and me. Rocco Malutki is standing beside her, tidying cups into the dishwasher.

But something about the picture is off.

There's aggression in the air.

Klatsche's noticed it too.

'Listen, guys,' he says, 'what's up?'

'What d'you mean,' says Rocco, 'why should anything be up?'

'What d'you mean,' says Carla, 'nothing's up.'

That was too quick, both of them were.

Now it's plain to see that something's very much up.

Carla sets two full-to-the-brim glasses of white wine down under Klatsche's nose and mine, bats her eyelashes and blasts out her sweetest smile.

Klatsche shakes his head and laughs.

And I say, 'Nope, nuh-uh, you can't kid a kidder. What the hell is up?'

'I have no idea what you mean,' says Carla, eyebrows as high as they'll go.

Rocco continues to focus his entire attention on the dishwasher, it looks like he's taking cover behind all the cups and glasses.

'Wait there,' says Klatsche, jumping up; a second later, he's in the cellar doorway. Rocco leaps out from behind the counter. He wants to hold Klatsche back, but he's already on the stairs. Rocco sprints after him.

'How nice, Carla,' I say, 'clearly everything is absolutely perfectly fine.'

She swears softly, and then Klatsche reappears on the cellar stairs.

'Chastity, could you come here a moment?'

I stand up, walk to the stairs and follow Klatsche down to the cellar. There are two chairs. Sitting on the chairs are two guys. The guys are back-to-back with their arms and legs tied to the chairs. Their mouths are gagged with black socks.

'What's all this,' I say, '*Pulp Fiction*?'

Rocco leans against the wall, looks at Klatsche and doesn't say a word. Klatsche lights a cigarette, drags hard and hands it to me.

'I think I know who they are,' he says.

'Yes,' I say, 'it's pretty safe to assume that it's them.'

The two men have their eyes open wide, one's desperately trying to talk to me. I ignore him and keep smoking.

'Explanation, please,' I say to Rocco.

Rocco rubs his hand over his chin.

'Yesterday night, they happened to bump into a couple of my mates,' he says.

'Aha,' says Klatsche. 'Happened to.'

'Bumped into a couple of your mates,' I say, 'well, fancy that, what are the chances?'

I drag on my cigarette.

'And then you didn't know what to do with the arseholes so you decided to store them down here for a while, until they start to rot? Or did Carla want to have the balls off them in peace, at some point this evening?'

The two men flinch, one of them, the big, strong one, starts whimpering.

Rocco raises his hands and pulls an ultra-innocent face.

'Stay here,' I tell Klatsche. 'I'm going to talk to Carla.'

I give him the cigarette and go up. Carla is standing between the cellar door and the bar, hands on hips.

'This is my business,' she says, 'keep out of it.'

'Carla,' I say, 'this is false imprisonment. You could go to jail.'

'Not if you keep your mouth shut,' she says.

'I'm a public prosecutor. I can't just keep my mouth shut.'

She digs her hands into her dark curls.

'That stupid cop-woman hasn't done a bloody thing,' she says, 'didn't give a flying fuck that those bastards were still running around out there, I waited ten days for something to happen, I kept calling and asking if they'd got anything, and they just kept saying that it was ongoing. But I swear they hadn't lifted a finger.'

'Carla,' I say, 'this kind of thing never goes that quickly.'

'Oh really? On Sunday evening, Rocco asked a couple of people if they could help us. And by this morning, two raping bastards were tied up in my cellar.'

I shake my head.

'I have to call the police.'

'Chastity, please,' she says, 'I know what we've done here doesn't look good, and then maybe they'll stop believing me, and they'll let them go. And you can't seriously believe that I'm the only person they've done that to. They're animals. They have no empathy. They treat women like shit. They'll do it again.'

I put my hands on her shoulders.

'They'll get what's coming to them,' I say, 'for sure. I promise you that. And you won't get into trouble.'

I go into the cellar, discuss exactly what to say with Klatsche and Rocco, and then I call my colleagues who deal with this stuff.

It takes a while for them to get here. I don't know if I'm being influenced by Carla, but the gentlemen seem a little bit feeble to me, as they listen to my watertight explanation for why the situation is the way it is: Carla's had this secret admirer for years. Someone from the Kiez. She doesn't know who he is, she doesn't know his name, she doesn't know what he looks like. She only knows from hearsay that he must be part of the criminal community. She's never even seen the man, but the whole Kiez is gossiping about it behind her back. And her admirer likes to give her somewhat dubious gifts. She tells someone that some idiot skipped out without paying, and the very next day, that same idiot has a black eye. She jokingly complains to her pals that one of her neighbours always bags the parking space outside her flat and – *wham* – his fancy Audi A8 gets nicked. And that must have been what happened to the rapists. She told the wrong people. And the lads promptly found their way, bound and gagged, into her cellar. A present, you know. So obviously, Carla rang me right away. She was in a total panic, poor thing. Such a panic. You can just imagine it.

My genius colleagues are clearly not one bit embarrassed that it wasn't them but this secret admirer who nicked the guys who assaulted Carla. Officially, that is.

And they're rather more concerned that somebody might have hurt these two delinquents.

Shit, shit, shit. I should have let Carla get on with it.

BETTER OUT THAN IN

Sadly, we failed to get past the red lantern again – that keeps on happening to us. We have every intention of going home but then there's this light on outside the Nachthafen. By day, it's a plain, white, opaque glass lantern above an unremarkable pub door at the end of a short flight of steps. Totally unassuming; it's easy to walk by. But as soon as dusk falls, the lamp starts to glow. Its light is a pale red, almost a touch pink. The colour that comic book characters' cheeks go when they fall in love. The lantern doesn't beam. It doesn't cast any light. It doesn't even light anything up. It looks incredibly content.

Perhaps that's what attracts us so strongly, we want to be part of that contentment for a few hours.

So now I'm sitting at the bar in the Nachthafen with a double vodka on the rocks in front of me, Klatsche pretty much inhaled his first beer and he's just ordering a second. Our discussions with Carla and Rocco were tiring, I feel worn and beige. I launch into my vodka and take a big gulp.

'Calling the cops was the right thing to do,' says Klatsche.

'No,' I say. 'It was wrong. I could slap myself all the way from here to Berlin.'

Carla wouldn't have killed the men.

'Carla just wanted to give those two guys a bit of a fright,' I say, 'which is only fair.'

'And she'd probably have hurt them a bit too,' says Klatsche. 'Or let them get hurt. Rocco knows a bunch of guys who have no nerves. It could have escalated quickly.'

'So what,' I say. 'Those scumbags hurt her first.'

'Since when have you been the eye-for-an-eye type?'

I down my vodka.

'Since today,' I say.

I order another vodka and a beer, and Klatsche gets another too. I'm in the mood for drinking, not talking.

He takes my head in his hands, gives me a kiss on the top of the head and then drinks his beer and leaves me in peace. These are the times.

At some point between our third and fourth beers, Klatsche's twenty-four-hour-locksmith-service phone rings. He answers it, making a huge effort to sound sober.

'I see,' he says. 'Is it locked?'

He looks at me and rolls his eyes.

'OK, where?'

He takes a felt-tip off the bar and writes an address on his hand.

'Fine, I'll be with you in ten minutes.'

He hangs up, slips off the stool and grabs his jacket.

'Lost keys,' he says. 'And a double-locked door. And there's a security bar with another four locks on it too. You'll have to carry on without me.'

'Are you planning to drive?'

'Obviously,' he says. 'But don't grass me up to the cops, OK?'

'You little sod,' I say.

'Love you too,' he says.

Luckily, I can drink perfectly well alone. I order another double vodka and a large glass of water, drink up the water and push my stool away from the bar and against the wall, lean back, hold on tight to my vodka and watch the disco ball. Watch it throwing little glittering squares onto the dark-red silk wallpaper. I shut my eyes and listen to the music, Screamin' Jay Hawkins, which somehow always hits the spot.

'Good evening.'

I open my eyes and it takes me a moment to place the woman.

'Jules Thomsen,' she says, 'remember me?'

'Oh, yes, of course,' I say. 'I'm sorry.'

'Hey, it's late,' she says, sending an understanding smile in my direction. She's immediately twigged that I'm no longer broadcasting on all frequencies.

'I'll get myself something and we can drink together,' she says.

OK, wow.

'I've got a major head start tonight,' I say.

'You don't know who you're up against,' she says, then she orders and I'm stunned. She's asked for a beer, a corn schnapps and a double gin and tonic.

'Not bad,' I say.

'*Prost*,' she says, and the *korn* is gone. Then, three, two, one, the beer. All while still standing. She seems to have left herself a little more time for the gin. She pushes a bar stool up to the wall beside me, leans back, lets the detergent get to work on her brain and says: 'I hate my job.'

'You make people stuff to eat,' I say, 'that's amazing.'

'Yeah, it could be wonderful,' she says, 'if I was doing it properly in a proper restaurant for customers I like.'

I sip my vodka, light a cigarette and hand her one too.

'Thanks,' she says. 'You know, I've just done another ten-hour day in the kitchen. In my own kitchen, in my own restaurant, and it fucks me off. Everything we're doing there is for show. It's all fake. It's chi-chi. It's way overpriced and thick as pig shit. Nobody needs that stuff.

It's shithead food for shitheads. I'm wasting my talent. I hate cooking for those people.'

'OK, listen here, you might be cooking for shitheads but that doesn't make it shithead food.'

'Yes it does.'

'So why do you do it?'

And why is she telling me all this?

'It just sort of happened,' she says. 'Somehow it just sort of happened. I'm sorry, I didn't mean to chew your ears off.'

'No worries. Better out than in.'

She drains her glass and orders another gin.

'What are you drinking then?'

'Vodka,' I say.

'I'll have one of those too please,' she says to the barman.

I'm not sure if I should drink any more, but I order another one anyway.

'I really ought to just sell the place and get the hell out of there,' she says.

'But?' I ask.

'I don't have time,' she says. 'I work such long hours that I don't even have time to stop.'

Our drinks come.

'*Prost.*'

'*Prost,*' I say.

'How about you?' she asks.

'What about me?' I ask. It won't be long before I'm seeing two chefs here.

'Do you like your job?'

'Most of the time,' I say. 'But not today.'

I drink up my vodka and twizzle the next glass between my fingers.

'Why not?'

'Because,' I say, 'I'm starting to doubt whether I'm still on the right side.'

'Then switch sides,' she says.

'Then sell your restaurant,' I say.

She looks at me and I look at her, and then she holds up her glass and we toast each other again, and then we listen to as much of Screamin' Jay Hawkins as we can, and then my mind loses the thread.

She's amazed that it's so simple, that it's so easy, that just a little bit of training gets results so quickly. Three weeks ago, she was still scared of every man who crossed her path. But she's just tried out that kick. The trainer was right. You don't need much strength. You just need a bit of speed and good aim.

Yes.

And now there's a guy lying here on the ground, in the middle of the pavement. This is a dark corner and it's way past midnight, nobody's going to come past anytime soon. All the same, she supposes that she'll have to do something. She can't just leave him lying here. Is he dead? What should she say when she calls the police? That he spoke to her? That he called her 'slut'? And then she straight-out killed him? By accident? Should she say that?

Doesn't sound good.

She thinks for a moment, then she does what women do in tricky situations. She calls her best friend.

That was so easy too, with two of them. Get the dead man in the car, get the dead man out of the car through the back door into the empty kitchen, hang the dead man up in the cold store. Nobody will spot anything. Nobody but the head chef is allowed in the cold store. So nobody else has a key to it. On principle. Which means that you can store stuff there if you're the boss. And the boss is now going to take personal charge of making everything disappear. The heads, hands and feet are disposed of. The rest will be processed, the way you do with any other pig.

The chef often makes the sausages overnight, when the kitchen is hers alone. Or marinates the meat, so that it can really steep. Or gets the ragu going, ready for the next day. The longer a ragu can simmer away to itself, the better.

Good prep is important to the chef, good produce, good spices, no ready-made blends or bought-in stuff like you find in other kitchens.

Most of the time these days, you just have no idea what you're eating, what's in the food.

Set Menu

Starters

Crostini with liver forcemeat and green grapes

Buffalo mozzarella with boiled rosemary ham

Mini salsicce lucane with black pepper
and marinated peperoncini

Wilted lettuce with porcini

Mains

Orecchiette al ragù in amarone

Jailbird Truffles – homemade meatballs
with potato and gherkin salad

Oven-baked roulades with plum and coriander
in a tamarind jus

Gentleman's Delight – salsiccia with fried potatoes

Oxtail ragù alla Cavour with butter gnocchi

Marsala schnitzel with fresh fennel

French-style black pudding
with apples and marjoram toast

Desserts

Cherry sponge cake with vanilla milk foam and macaron

Dark chocolate-coated chestnuts

She's walking through the city. She's looking for someone. Someone who'll get funny with her. Who'll hit on her. Someone she can sock it to, kick in the face. It's time for another arsehole to get a kicking. They all deserve it. They're all the same.

She walks and walks and walks.

She's wearing her extra-short skirt, just to make sure. That way, someone's bound to come and hit on her. They always come and hit on her.

There. Him over there.

He's coming towards her. He looks at her. He seems nice. Young, polite, well brought up. She knows that that's just a façade. He's not fooling her. This is a dark corner, you don't talk to a woman around here. Doesn't that occur to them? That the woman will feel scared if they talk to her around here? That she has no choice but to defend herself?

Excuse me, he says, do you have a light, please?

Pow, game over, mate.

Smoked out.

ACTUALLY

Oh ye gods and little fishes, my skull aches. And how exactly am I supposed to open my eyes, I can hear Klatsche talking somewhere, but I couldn't say where, what about or why. What's he even doing here? We didn't even come home together last night. Did we? I try to lift my head. Can't be done. At least I've grasped the fact that Klatsche's on the phone now. I think he's getting closer. Wow, that's loud. When he finally, finally, hangs up, I cautiously activate my voice.

'What are you doing here?'

'Good God,' he says, 'it speaks.'

I turn onto my belly, lean on my elbows and grip my head. Holy moly.

'Ow,' I say.

Klatsche sits down next to me on the bed and holds out a glass. There's water in the glass and it's fizzing.

'Here, aspirin.'

I actually manage to sit up, take the glass and drink.

'What are you doing here?' I ask again.

'You're asking me what I'm doing in my own flat?'

'What?'

'We're in my flat, you numpty.'

'Why?'

'I picked you up off the front doorstep,' he says, 'when I got home after doing my locksmith bit. You were having, shall we say, a few difficulties.'

I let myself fall back into the pillow. My body feels like someone coated it in tar then poured it out.

'Can I have a coffee?'

'Of course you can have a coffee.'

Everything happened so fast yesterday. I can hold my drink really, it's not like that, but the pace that that Jules Thomsen was setting was superhuman. I roll onto my side and look out of the window. Yep. Klatsche's place. You can't see out of the window at all from my bed.

And suddenly there's this woman in my head.

She's got dark-blonde curls. At first, I can't remember where I'm getting her from, but then memory slowly dawns. She stumbled into the Nachthafen later on. Drank a quick vodka with us. She was a friend of Jules Thomsen's, that's right. She came in, seriously worked up about something but I didn't get what it was all about. And then she snaffled my drinking buddy. She literally dragged her out of the pub.

But I'm not sure.

ROSES AND LIGHTHOUSES

I'm slowly getting going again, I'm ensconced behind my files at the prosecution service, still pretty much on the ropes, but at least I'm capable of holding a telephone now.

I phone Faller, that old rose-pruner. It rings three times before he answers.

'Chastity,' he says, 'nice of you to call.'

'Nice of you to answer,' I say. 'How are you?'

'Super, thank you.'

'How come?'

A Faller with nothing to complain about is unheard of.

'I finally cut back my roses,' he says.

The roses again.

'I put it off for so long, but now the dead wood is gone, I don't have to worry about it anymore, which feels great.'

I don't think Faller's talking about his roses at all.

'You don't need the lighthouse anymore?'

'Well now,' Faller says, 'you can never be entirely sure about that, of course.'

I light a cigarette.

'Could you spare me a little time, then?'

'Of course, my girl,' he says. 'When?'

'This evening? Dinner?'

'Where?' he asks.

I can't help remembering yesterday evening. Jules Thomsen and her hatred for her fancy joint. I'd like to take another look at the place.

'Let's go to Taste.'

'To what?' he asks.

'That restaurant in the old factory building,' I say. 'Just off the Reeperbahn. You know?'

'Not a clue,' he says.

'Well, come and pick me up from home at eight then.'

'I'll come and pick you up from home at eight then.'

Faller in the disco restaurant. Fabulous.

STAFF ONLY

He holds the menu up to his face. Sometimes he pulls it down a fraction so that all I can see are his eyes. I bet he's pulling faces at me behind it.

'Did you eat a clown for breakfast?'

He pulls the menu down to his chin and says, 'Sorry, but this place is hilarious. "Pierced perch", I mean, come on, this is bullshit. If you'll tell me why we're here, I'm all ears.'

'Just because,' I say, 'no particular reason. I thought it would be fun to sit around in here and see what happens.'

'Ha-ha, Chastity.'

Our waiter's name is Bengt, and Bengt looks pretty much exactly the same as Jason. He brings Faller a water and me a glass of white wine. Then he starts rattling off the day's specials. Jason didn't do that.

I'm not really a fan of these things, but maybe I should try the black pudding. Jules Thomsen said the sausage here was something special. I'd like to know what she meant.

'I'll have the black pudding and apple,' I say.

'And I'll have the Jailbird Truffles,' says Faller.

Bengt nods.

'Jailbird Truffles?' I ask.

'Meatballs, apparently,' says Faller. '*Frikadellen*. They're not so easy to do well. And really out of character for this place. Let's see if they're up to it.'

'They're up to it,' I say.

'How d'you know that?' he says. 'Come here often?'

'No,' I say, 'but I met the head chef recently and I kind of like her.'

'You like a woman who runs a place like this? Are you serious, Chas?'

I lean across the table and say quietly: 'She hates the place. She hates the location and the people. But somehow, she can't ditch the joint.'

'Now that, on the other hand,' says Faller, 'I can really sympathise with. To be trapped in your own life and be able to admit it. Not many people can do that.'

'Yes,' I say, 'most people would keep pretending everything was great, wouldn't they?'

Faller nods, sips his water and looks pensively at me.

'So, now let's talk about the thing we're here about,' he says. 'What's up with the dead men dredged out of the Elbe? Problems?'

'Yeah,' I say, 'difficult. Up until the day before yesterday, we had practically nothing to get our teeth into. Calabretta was pretty much investigating by way of shots in the dark, it was driving him nuts, he was pulling all-nighters, watching out at random for anyone acting suspiciously, just for something to do. And now suddenly we've got a witness. But he's a weirdo. We suspect he's ha-rassing a woman, stalking her. But even so, he probably saw her kill someone who looked pretty much exactly like our first victim. And he saw a second woman too.'

Faller looks at me. His expression says: I knew it. Two women.

'But it sounds more like manslaughter than murder, in the heat of the moment,' I say. 'It might even have been self-defence. But that's really not in keeping with the first two victims being dismembered and packaged up in bin bags. And anyway – three victims? That makes no sense.'

Faller scratches his chin.

'This witness,' he asks. 'Could he give a decent descrip-tion of the women?'

'The photofits we made with his help are useless,' I say. 'The guy either couldn't or wouldn't tell us anything spe-cific. Even so, Calabretta's sent a bunch of guys out into the Kiez to keep an eye out, round the clock, for a woman with dark-blonde curls and racy curves.'

'For someone like her?'

He glances over at the bar. There's that waitress, the one I noticed last time. It's like there's a dust cloud of sex billowing around her, and in any place that a man's eyes fall on her, the dust particles start to glitter. The air flickers with every step she takes and today that seems to be making her particularly grumpy.

'Yeah,' I say, 'pretty much.'

'Poor woman,' says Faller, 'every bloke in this room will get himself off to sleep thinking about her.'

'But she won't know that,' I say.

'Yes she will,' says Faller. 'She's perfectly aware of it. Look at the way she squirms beneath their gaze ... Wouldn't surprise me if she gets grabbed by some arsehole once an evening.'

I watch the waitress. Faller's probably right. I can't tell. I don't know what it's like when men look at you like that, they never look at me like that, they're more likely to be afraid of me.

At the other end of the restaurant, the swing door to the kitchen opens and I see Jules Thomsen walk out. She stops very close to the door and scans the room intently. She seems to be looking for someone. And then the waitress with the curls joins her, and it's only then that I twig that she must be the woman from last night, Jules's friend, **the one who came rushing in, who was so worked up.**

It's clear that the women are close. There's trust and soul between them, in the way they look at each other and talk to each other and keep taking each other's hands in a casual way. With love, care, great understanding for each other. I've gone all warm around the eyes.

'Black pudding for the lady,' says Bengt, 'and meatballs for sir, here you are.'

'Thank you,' says Faller.

And in the moment that the plates of food are set on the table in front of us, something happens in my head. It feels like a circuit where one fuse after another is switched on, like one light after another is starting to glow, bright and clear. One after another, images drop through my brain.

The dead faces of Dejan Pantelic and Jürgen Rost.

The hands, the feet, neatly packaged.

Sonny von Lell.

Brückner, saying that the three men treated women with disrespect.

The kick that killed the men.

The waitress's feline body tension.

Her rage last night.

Jules Thomsen's rage.

The contempt she feels for her customers.

And the tender way she recognised that Carla had been hurt. Like she was familiar with such things.

And then this food.

Meat.

Lupara bianca, Calabretta called it – making the bodies disappear by throwing them to the pigs.

'Faller,' I say.

He sticks his fork into his meatball and cuts off a piece.

'Looks amazing,' he says.

'Faller. Don't eat that.'

'Why not? That's why we're here, isn't it?'

'Maybe I'm insane,' I say, 'maybe I'm completely insane, but please: don't eat that.'

I try to ignore the black pudding on my plate, but it's like it's continually pushing its way into my field of vision, as if it's forcing me to look at it. I feel sick. I stand up and walk towards the toilets, the room around me blurs before my eyes, starts spinning, I hold my hand to my mouth, just about make it to the bowl, and then it's not nice at all, my body turns itself inside out, I'm spewing building blocks.

When it's over, I pull myself up on the wash basin and get a shock at the sight of the woman in the mirror. I wash my face with cold water and try to wipe away the dark rings under my eyes with my fingers.

'You've got it all wrong,' I tell my reflection, take a deep breath and stroke my hair out of my face again, and on the way back into the restaurant, I spot this door in the long, red-painted corridor. *Staff Only. No Access to Customers.*

The door is open and leads to an inner courtyard, there's a paved path across the courtyard, to either side of which is a tiny patch of grass, framed by a few clumps of bamboo. On the lawn are large pebbles, rounded as if they'd been polished by the waves. They're exactly the right size. The paved path leads to a sliding grille, behind which is a commercial bin. The grille is closed, but I can climb over it. I open the bin. It's full to the brim with thick, black sacks.

I close the container again and climb back through into the yard. There's another door, and this one leads directly into the kitchen.

Jules Thomsen is standing at one of the four gas hobs. She's taking sausages off a hook and placing them in a heavy cast-iron pan, the finished dishes are on a long table, ready to be carried out by the waiting staff. Aha, I think. Black pudding's clearly popular today. But the bratwurst is too, as are some things that look like spiced, marinated cutlets. And then there are the meatballs, like the ones Faller had on his plate.

There's a large pan on another gas ring. Simmering away in the pan is a thick ragu. I can't see what's in the three ovens. But I can smell it: meat.

Jules looks at me. She takes her friend's hand, the friend

who has just come through the other door into the kitchen. The friend looks at me too.

There are precisely fifteen people in this kitchen, but only two women know what happened here. A third is just starting to catch on.

I come to stand beside Jules and her friend at the hob. They look at me the way Carla looked at me when I came out of her cellar: keep out of this, this is our affair.

They know that I can guess what they did.

'Hey, Jules,' I say.

She is holding tightly on to her pan with one hand and her friend with the other.

'You asked me yesterday if I like my job,' I say. 'Do you remember?'

She nods.

I take a deep breath, then I lean in a bit closer to the two friends so that, in a moment, when I speak very softly, they'll be able to hear me.

Everyone else in the kitchen is ignoring me. The arrogance of those at work.

'I'm a public prosecutor,' I say, 'and there are situations where I don't like my job.'

Jules lets go of the pan and holds on to the hob.

'There are times when I feel like I'm being remote-controlled, like I have no freedom of choice.'

She's still holding her friend's hand.

'Like, for instance,' I say, 'when I realise that I really need to get out of here. Far away. If I have a sudden urge to take a holiday in Rio or Buenos Aires or Mexico City. If I get the feeling that I want to be so far away that nobody can find me.'

The two women stare at me, the rest of the kitchen just keeps on working.

'Then the fact that I can't just do that really gets on my nerves. You can't be spontaneous when you work for the state. You have to put in for leave a long way in advance, and it has to be approved, and by then it's usually too late, my itchy feet have settled down.'

I pull out my cigarettes, light one and hold out the packet to the two of them. Jules takes one, I give her a light. Her friend shakes her head.

'I really wish I had more options,' I say, dragging on my cigarette and staring at the ceiling lights. 'Especially right now when the weather's about to change – they say it's going to get really sticky in Hamburg. You know, if I could, I'd make a break for it as soon as possible. Take the next flight to South America, for example, or the next boat.'

'OK,' says Jules.

What am I even saying, I think, as I reply, 'OK.'

We finish our cigarettes in peace, and then I throw the

butt into the pan of ragu and leave the way I came, through the backyard, through the door by the toilets, through the restaurant, back to Faller at the table and sit down. He hasn't touched his food.

'Everything OK?'

'Yes,' I say, 'everything's OK.'

Or at least that's how it feels.

'Can we eat now then?' asks Faller.

'No,' I say. 'We shouldn't eat that.'

'What the hell, Chastity? I could eat a horse, and these meatballs look seriously tasty.'

'I'll buy you a currywurst later,' I say. 'First we'll step outside and have a smoke, and then when we've finished that, we're going to call Calabretta.'

Faller shakes his head, lays his napkin on the table and stands up.

'A man can't even have dinner in peace with you around,' he says. 'But if you say so, then fine by me.'

I down my wine in one, beckon that Bengt over and press a hundred into his hand.

Outside the door, I light two cigarettes and hand one to Faller. We smoke. He pushes his hat back a notch. The hat is pale grey and looks very clean. Faller blows clouds of smoke into the dusk and watches me out of the corner of his eye.

'Chastity?'

'Yes.'

'Didn't you want to call Calabretta?'

'Yes, I did.'

'When?'

'When I've finished my smoke,' I say.

'Listen, I don't know what's going on here, but I know that *something* is going on.'

'So?'

'So, nothing,' he says, throwing the cigarette I gave him into the gutter, pulling a packet of Roth-Händle out of his trouser pocket and lighting one.

'Nice hat,' I say. 'Is it new?'

'Yes,' he says, 'I bought it yesterday.'

I drag on my cigarette and blow the smoke onto his brim.

DAMMIT

We really should have got the descriptions out sooner.

THE BEER AND THE CIGARETTES

It was Klatsche's idea. He says he always used to do this with his mates, when they were fifteen, sixteen or so. A couple of cans of beer per person, a packet of cigarettes to share and then head out to the airport to watch the planes.

We're sitting on the viewing terrace. They're kind of playing at bistros here, with their round white tables and fancy plastic chairs. They're not too pleased to see us with our cans, but we don't care, we drink the beer and smoke the cigarettes and bid one plane after another farewell as they vanish into the sky. The clouds are several layers deep and moving fast.

Suddenly, it smells of autumn. It's often like that here when the weather breaks.

'Maybe that was it for summer,' I say.

'Doesn't matter,' says Klatsche, crushing his beer can and opening another. 'Want to go away for the weekend?'

'I don't know.'

'In two hours, there's a flight to Glasgow,' he says, 'it's

kind of like Hamburg. Wouldn't be so much of a shock to your system.'

I've got ancestors from Glasgow, so strictly speaking, I have family there.

'Scotland,' I say. 'Actually, why not?'

We drink up, go in and buy two toothbrushes.

'Jules?'

'Suzanna?'

'Pass the suncream please.'

'Face or body?'

'Face.'

'Here you go.'

'Thanks.'

'Another daiquiri?'

'Daiquiri, sheesh.'

'What?'

'I don't know how you can keep downing all that strong drink.'

'Oh, you know, only the strong survive etc. etc.'

'The weakest go to the wall, etc. etc.'

'Don't go telling me that you're weak.'

'I was weak once.'

'I know.'

ACKNOWLEDGEMENTS

A massive THANK YOU goes to:

All the fantastic women in my life.